P9-APD-697

"I don't want your money," Keir said

Regan could feel her heart beating in her throat. "Then what do you want?"

"You." His voice was hard. "I want you, Regan. I always have."

She stared at him in utter dismay. "You can't be serious," she whispered. "We had a bargain, Keir."

"We got married," he retorted. "That gives me certain unassailable rights."

"It does not!" There was a spark in her eyes now. "Whatever you have in mind, you can forget it, do you hear? This is *my* house, *my* home. I want you out of here!"

"I'm your husband," Keir said flatly. "I'm staying. Reconcile yourself to that fact, Regan. You're going to give me what I want in the end—and I don't care how long it takes."

KAY THORPE
is also the author of these

Harlequin Presents

and these

Harlequin Romances

Many of these titles are available at your local bookseller.

For a free catalogue listing all available Harlequin Romances and Harlequin Presents, send your name and address to:

HARLEQUIN READER SERVICE,
1440 South Priest Drive, Tempe, AZ 85281
Canadian address: Stratford, Ontario N5A 6W2

KAY THORPE

temporary marriage

Harlequin Books

TORONTO • LONDON • LOS ANGELES • AMSTERDAM
SYDNEY • HAMBURG • PARIS • STOCKHOLM • ATHENS • TOKYO

Harlequin Presents edition published March 1982
ISBN 0-373-10491-X

Original hardcover edition published in 1981
by Mills & Boon Limited

Copyright © 1981 by Kay Thorpe. All rights reserved.
Philippine copyright 1981. Australian copyright 1981.
Cover illustration copyright © 1982 by Fred Oakley.
Except for use in any review, the reproduction or utilization of
this work in whole or in part in any form by any electronic,
mechanical or other means, now known or hereafter invented,
including xerography, photocopying and recording, or in any
information storage or retrieval system, is forbidden without
the permission of the publisher, Harlequin Enterprises Limited,
225 Duncan Mill Road, Don Mills, Ontario, Canada M3B 3K9.

All the characters in this book have no existence outside the
imagination of the author and have no relation whatsoever to
anyone bearing the same name or names. They are not even
distantly inspired by any individual known or unknown to the
author, and all the incidents are pure invention.

The Harlequin trademark, consisting of the words
HARLEQUIN PRESENTS and the portrayal of a Harlequin,
is registered in the United States Patent Office and in the
Canada Trade Marks Office.

Printed in U.S.A.

CHAPTER ONE

IT was snowing when Regan emerged from Matthew Swain's office, large, drifting flakes which threatened to stick and cover in a very short time. On impulse she crossed the road to the Old House Café, taking a table in the window and smiling a response to the waitress's friendly greeting as the latter came over with order pad poised.

'Just tea and hot toast, please, Edith,' she said. 'And do you have the time? I left my watch at home.'

'It's just gone four, Miss O'Neil,' returned the woman pleasantly. 'Goes dark so early on days like this, doesn't it? Hope we're not going to have as bad a winter as they're all saying—it makes things so difficult.'

'For everyone,' Regan agreed. 'I'm afraid they're probably right, though. Barlow's been forecasting it since the holly first came into berry.'

'And he's hardly ever wrong,' the other woman sighed. 'Oh well, we'll just have to put up with it, won't we? Only another two months or so and we'll be into spring.'

And in little more than one month she would be twenty-five, acknowledged Regan as the waitress went to place her order. Five weeks in which to find herself a husband or lose the home she loved so dearly. True, she could always contest the will, as Matt had suggested this afternoon, but even if she could bring herself to drag the family name through the appeal courts it was surely a little late for that now. Three years ago the condition had not seemed nearly so unreasonable. Most girls were married by the time they were twenty-five anyway. The trouble was she had never found any

5

man she wanted to marry—not enough, at any rate. Perhaps now might be a good time to start reviewing past offers, because she didn't have long in which to start looking around for new ones.

The man who had come into the café almost on her heels had taken a table a short distance away, his dark overcoat slung over a spare chair. Regan could feel his eyes on her now and kept hers averted just far enough to avoid catching his gaze. She was accustomed enough to attracting male attention to know just how little encouragement it took to have them fancying their chances at striking up a conversation. Right now the last thing she wanted was company of any kind. She had to think.

The hot fragrant tea was a comfort. Holding the cup between her hands, she looked out of the window at the whirling flakes and recalled the gist of the letter her father had left her on his death.

Cottam needs a family, he had written, *and I look to you to provide it with one of your own. If you still haven't settled down by the time you're twenty-five I somehow doubt that you ever really will, so I've made provision for the Manor to be sold in those circumstances and the proceeds invested along with the trust fund to provide you with an income adequate to almost any life-style you choose to live until your thirtieth birthday, when you come into full control of the whole estate. Always remember that I love you, and want only what is best for you.*

What he had *thought* was best for her, Regan tagged on wryly. She had loved her father too, but they had not always seen eye to eye. No one could lay down rules for living in black and white. Cottam had been in the family for three generations. Why should she be deprived of it as a home simply because she couldn't find a man she could love in any lasting fashion?

Backed by the gathering darkness outside, the glass of the window showed a clear reflection of the café behind her. Without realising it, she had been watching the man at the nearby table, responding to the pull of his eyes on her. Now, seeing him rise suddenly to his feet, she was aware of a tiny little quiver deep down inside her—a sense of recognition. Where had she seen that litheness of movement before, that tall, broad-shouldered frame?

He was coming over, she realised. She made herself turn her head slowly as he came to a stop beside the table, looking up a long way into a pair of grey eyes which gave nothing away. His hair was dark and crisply cut, his features even, though too strongly moulded to be called handsome. Not a face to forget easily, and she hadn't forgotten. She never had been able to forget.

'Hallo, Keir,' she said. 'It's been a long time.'

He made no immediate reply, studying the smooth pure oval of a face uptilted towards him; the small straight nose, wide-spaced green eyes and full mouth framed by the fall of coppery hair. A faint ironic smile touched his lips.

'Almost six years,' he agreed. 'I wasn't sure you'd remember me. You've changed very little, Regan. I knew you the moment I saw you crossing the road out there.' He paused then as if in expectancy, brows lifting a fraction when she failed to respond. 'Mind if I sit down?'

'Please do,' she invited, seeing no way out of it. Her smile was bright and forced. 'I thought you were in Australia. Didn't you emigrate?'

'That's right.' There was a sudden spark in the grey eyes, fleeting but disturbing. 'A fresh start seemed advisable at the time.'

Her glance held a swift and almost unconscious appraisal of the cut of his tweed jacket. 'A successful one, I take it?'

'Moderately.' His tone was dismissive. 'How's your father?'

Her face stiffened, the smile fading. 'He died three years ago. It's just me now.'

'All alone in that big house?'

'Apart from the staff, yes.'

'That's a pity,' he said. 'A real pity. If ever a house called out for a family it's Cottam.'

Shut up! she wanted to tell him, but she didn't, sitting there instead with a frozen expression and a wish for him to be gone. Once, long ago, this man had asked her to marry him and she had turned him down. Not just turned him down but laughed in his face at the very idea that she might even consider marrying the son of a local postman. He was mocking her now, deliberately reminding her of what was past and gone. Only she wasn't going to let him discomfit her. Not in any fashion.

'I'm not the family type,' she came back levelly. 'I prefer my own company when *I* choose to have it.'

'No ties, no restrictions?' His tone was soft. 'Maybe you're right at that.'

'You're married?' she asked without meaning to, and saw the dark head move in negation.

'Never found the time. Could be I had the inclination shot right out of me.'

Another dig, but she still refused to react. 'I should be getting back,' she said, reaching for her purse. 'The weather isn't going to improve.'

'Running away?' he suggested as she half rose to her feet, and she paused in the act to look at him, features controlled.

'No, I'm not running away. I don't have anything to run from.'

'Then stay and finish your tea. I'll order fresh for us both."

Meeting the challenge in the grey eyes, Regan found herself slowly sitting down again, aware that in doing so she was acknowledging a will stronger than her own yet somehow reluctant to assert herself. She had treated Keir Anderson abominably in the past. The least she could do to make amends was to stay and be pleasant to him now when it no longer mattered.

'Are you back in England for good?' she asked when the tea was ordered, trying for a suitably light note of interest.

'Just on a visit,' he returned. 'I found myself in the Midlands, so I decided to look up old haunts for a couple of days. I'm staying at the Bull's Head. That hasn't changed much either.'

'Six years isn't long,' she defended. 'I daresay the town hasn't altered all that much in the last fifty.'

'Apart from its population. I spent yesterday trying to find a few old friends, but apart from Jake Carter they've all left for pastures new.'

'I stayed on,' she pointed out, and saw his lips twist again.

'Hardly the same thing. We lived on different levels—as you said at the time.'

Shame stirred in her, prompting an impulsive gesture. 'I was an awful little snob in those days.'

'Only when it came to marrying below your station,' Keir responded equably. 'After all, we had a fairly close relationship for several weeks.'

Regan needed no reminder. She could remember it all. Keir had been so different from the other young men of her aquaintance. At twenty-four he had possessed an initiative and drive which drew her to him even against her will. She had never really intended the association to go beyond that first casual date made when, bored out of her mind one evening at a local disco, she had accepted his invitation to dance. Her own crowd had viewed the whole affair with varied reactions, some amused, some resentful, some openly critical. She hadn't cared a whit for any opinion, intent only on her own personal enjoyment. Keir had taken her places she had never been before, talked about things no one else ever bothered to discuss—kissed her with a passion that stirred new depths in her, yet he never once attempted to overstep the limits of her eighteen-year-old emotions. She had known full well how he felt about her, and made no effort to stave off his final and inevitable declaration. In effect, he had been just another scalp to hang at her belt. How could she have been so utterly self-centred?

'I'm sorry,' she said. 'I was wrong to treat you the way I did.'

'But not wrong to turn me down?'

Her chin lifted. 'I don't think so. We really had very little in common.'

'No?' The question was soft, his smile registering the fleeting reaction in her eyes. 'Well, maybe you're right at that. You were too used to having things your own way to fit in easily with my ideas. When a working-class wife steps out of line she gets put back into it pretty sharply. You wouldn't have liked that.'

He was mocking her again, but he was entitled. Regan laughed and shook her head. 'Not at all.'

The pause was lengthy. Keir was the first to break it, tone light and detached. 'So much for old times. How are the new?'

'Fine.' She was quick, but not quick enough. She knew he had seen the shift of expression in her face. Looking at him, she was struck by an idea so sudden and preposterous she almost laughed out loud. Yet the notion persisted. It would be a solution of a kind, though not necessarily with this man. Who else? Who did she know who might even consider such a step?

Keir was still watching her, eyes enigmatic. 'Something worrying you?'

It was out before she could stop it, born of some instinct she had no time to analyse. 'Yes, it is. I'm in a spot and I'm not sure how to get out of it.'

'Want to talk about it?'

Regan gazed at him for one uncertain moment before once more giving way to instinct. 'Not here. How about coming out to the house for dinner this evening?'

If he was surprised by the invitation he didn't show it. 'That sounds a good idea. The food at the Bull isn't exactly haute cuisine.'

What would he know of haute cuisine? she wondered, and immediately took herself to task. He had moved up in the world since the days when she had known him. Far enough at least to recognise the distinction between the good and the merely adequate.

'Are you still in engineering?' she asked, and saw his head incline.

'More or less. What time would you like me to come?'

'Make it around seven-thirty, then we can have a drink before we eat. I'll ask Mrs Sullivan to put on something special in honour of the occasion.'

'You keep a cook just for yourself?'

The censure was more imagined than apparent, but her response made no allowances. 'I entertain a lot,' she defended. 'And she's been at Cottam a long time.'

'I know. I remember her.' His tone was level. 'You've become over-sensitive, Regan. There was a time when you wouldn't have found it necessary to make any excuses.'

'We all change as we grow,' she said.

Keir's lips tilted. 'In some ways, perhaps. It will be interesting to find out just how far yours go.' He got to his feet before she could reply, taking a couple of notes from a supple leather wallet to lay on top of the bill. 'Seven-thirty it is. I'll look forward to it.'

She watched him move to pick up his coat and shrug into it, already regretting the invitation. Yet what did she have to lose? The idea still lingering at the back of her mind was only an idea. She didn't have to follow it through.

The gritters had been out on the main roads. It was only on taking the narrow lane up to the house that she encountered any difficulties in the thickening snow. There was a very good chance that Keir would be unable to make it this far tonight at all, she realised, turning in at last through the double iron gates. It hadn't occurred to her to ask him if he had transport, and the town's two taxi firms were notoriously reluctant to run the risk of having their vehicles stranded.

So let fate supply its own answer, she reasoned. If he didn't come then she would abandon the whole crazy idea. It would leave her right back where she had started, but that was something she would have to accept. She almost wished it would happen that way.

The house came into sight around the bend in the drive, the big, square façade brightly lit and welcoming. Much too large for one person, she had to admit, but given time she would eventually do something about that. What she didn't want was to lose the only home she had ever known for reasons as unfair as those her father had imposed. Yet what was the alternative? Failing an appeal to the courts she was left with only one, and that might not even present itself.

Sullivan met her at the door, his well-worn features creasing into a relieved smile.

'I thought we were going to have to send out search parties,' he said. 'You said you'd be back by three.'

Regan returned the smile fondly, handing over her sheepskin coat. John Sullivan had been the family retainer for over thirty years, and in some ways almost took the place of the father she had lost. She would have been lost herself without him. Her father had made provision for any staff made redundant by the sale of the house, but no amount of money could compensate people like this man and his wife Ann for the deprivation of both jobs and home. Sullivan was too old to start again somewhere else, even if another position befitting his abilities could be found in this day and age. He would be forced into retirement at sixty-three, his wife at fifty-eight, because she certainly would not be prepared to take another post without him. In his cool, collected, businesslike way, her father had thought of everything but the feelings of those actually concerned.

'It took longer than I anticipated,' she said. 'I called in at the Old House for tea. Would you tell Mrs Sullivan we may have a guest at dinner tonight, provided he can get here. Not much point in going to any extra lengths on the chance that he does make it. Her steak Diane is always superb anyway.'

'Just one gentleman?' Sullivan sounded alert, aware as she was of the conditions governing his future employment. 'Anyone we know, Miss Regan?'

'Perhaps from a long time back.' There was little point in keeping the identity of her guest a secret. In Cottam everyone knew, or at least knew of, almost everyone else. 'He's Tom Anderson's son, Keir.'

'Anderson?' His brows drew together in the effort of recollection. 'I don't think——'

'You remember—Tom worked for the Post Office up until five years or so ago. He always came in for a lot of ridicule from some of the local men for letting his wife call their only son such an outlandish name.'

'Oh yes.' There was a subtle disappointment in the response. 'Went off to Australia after she died, didn't he?'

'To join his son. Keir's over here on holiday—at least that's the impression I got.'

'Odd time of year to choose for a holiday.'

'Oh, I don't know. They probably miss the winters out there.' Regan was leafing through the mail placed neatly on the central hall table tray as she spoke, flipping aside a couple of obvious bills. 'Was this all there was in the second delivery?'

Sullivan could have pointed out that the fact was fairly obvious, but he didn't. It would never have occurred to him to be that disrespectful. 'I'm afraid so,' he said. 'Were you expecting something important?'

'Not really,' she sighed. 'Just a faint hope that something might turn up. I can't even think what.'

'This—gentleman you're expecting,' Sullivan resumed, hesitating just long enough over the word. 'Is he—well, you know what I mean.'

Her smile came without volition. 'Sullivan, you're as big a snob still as I used to be,' she chided gently. 'Don't worry, he knows which knife and fork to use. He always did.'

'Always?' His brows had lifted in questioning surprise.

'Yes, I knew him before he went to Australia.' Her tone was wry. 'I treated him rather badly, as a matter of fact.'

'And now you want to make some amends.' He gave a nod of understanding. 'It's a very nice gesture, Miss Regan. I hope he appreciates it.'

'Oh, I'm sure he will.' She kept the dryness to herself. 'He's coming for seven-thirty, weather allowing. We'll eat around eight.'

'What if he gets here and can't get away again?' came the hesitant response, and she turned a bland face.

'Then he'll have to spend the night. Heaven knows, we've plenty of room. You might ask Mary to make up a bed just in case. The Blue Room, I think.'

'That's right next door to yours.' He sounded fairly shocked. 'Miss Regan——'

'I was only teasing,' she said penitently. 'I doubt if he'd be persuaded to stay under any circumstances.'

And rightly so, his expression said. He nodded,

relieved. 'I'll go and tell Mrs Sullivan.'

Going slowly upstairs, Regan viewed the darkness through the long Georgian window at the back and realised it had stopped snowing at last. The knowledge brought an oddly mixed reaction. If Keir came would she have the kind of raw courage necessary to her plan, or would her nerve fail her at the last moment? There was only one way to find out.

He arrived at a quarter to the hour, driving up to the door in a light-coloured Audi saloon. Looking down from the same long window, Regan saw him take the three steps lightly and heard the deep tone of the bell before composing herself for the descent to the hall. He was here and she was faced with the problem. To speak or not to speak. Which?

Sullivan was taking the same dark overcoat he had worn that afternoon, but under it Keir now had on a silver-grey suit that brought out his tan. She could see Sullivan's face as he turned away, and hid a grin, reading his thoughts with the accuracy of long acquaintance. Failing the ultimate perfection of a regular dinner suit, it was dark grey or blue only in his book of rules. No matter that such ideals were things of the past. For Sullivan nothing changed.

Her own choice of dress met with scarcely more approval. Too short and too tight, she could almost hear him thinking. She gave him an impish smile before going on past him to put out her hand to greet her guest.

'I'm glad you could make it. Good thing the snow stopped.'

'They're forecasting more,' Keir said easily. 'A whole lot of it, by all accounts.'

'Then you might have some difficulty getting back to town.'

His smile was slow. 'So we'll have to keep an eye on things, won't we? Did you say something about a drink? I'm feeling the cold.'

'Of course. This way.' She moved at his side, aware of his tallness, his leanness, the suggestion of controlled strength beneath the well-cut jacket. She found herself chattering on nervously, more unsure of herself than she ever remembered before in her life. 'I thought we'd use the library. It's cosier than the drawing room. It used to be Daddy's favourite place for an after-dinner brandy. Mostly I'd have my coffee in here too. We could do that tonight, if you'd like.'

'Why not?' He sounded amused. 'If we run out of conversation we can always read a good book.'

'Don't mock me!' she began with heat, and abruptly shut up, knowing she had asked for it. What was wrong with her anyway? No one was forcing her to do this thing. She could back out any time.

The library was softly lit, a small but comfortable room, its walls shelved in oak and packed to capacity with volumes of every shape and size. Two deep club chairs, a mahogany desk and a couple of occasional tables constituted the major furnishings. The Turkish carpet felt thick beneath their feet.

Regan waved a hand towards the drinks tray already set out on the desk top. 'Would you like to help yourself? I think you'll find a fair selection. If you want something else I can ring for Sullivan.'

'Scotch will do fine,' he said, lifting a bottle of Black Label to unscrew the cap with a sure hand. 'I thought this stuff was practically impossible to get hold of in this country.'

'I wouldn't know. I never touch it.' She waited until he had poured the double tot and restopped the bottle before saying evenly, 'I'll have a sherry, please. Medium dry.'

'Sorry.' Keir didn't turn a hair. 'Guess I wasn't thinking.'

She didn't believe that. He had purposely refrained

from asking her first. Why? she wondered. Simply for the pleasure of making her wait? It seemed unlikely, yet who was to know how Keir Anderson's mind moved these days? Six years ago he had let her in, given her his trust. And she had betrayed him. Could she blame him all that much now for feeling the way he obviously did? She was a spoiled baggage who needed putting in her place. Well, let him have his fun and games. They harmed no one, her least of all.

'Tell me about Australia,' she invited when they both had their glasses and a seat. 'I've never been there.'

He obliged readily enough, painting a lucid picture of the Sydney area and the surrounding countryside, yet keeping everything on a general level. Try as she might, she could get little out of him with regard to personal detail except that he was in the engineering line, which she already knew, and he travelled around the country quite a bit on business.

'How about your father?' she asked at last, giving up on the rest. 'Does he live with you?'

'Dad married again a couple of years back,' he said. 'They have their own home across the other side of town.'

'So you have a stepmother now.'

'Who, Alice?' His grin came swift and fleeting. 'She's about as motherly as a can of beans! A real tough old Sheila with a heart of gold, to use the vernacular. She's given Dad a new lease of life.'

'I'm glad.' Regan could think of nothing else to say. This was proving more difficult even than she had imagined. They had nothing to fall back on, no common ground. The past was taboo, she had already decided that, but what did it leave?

Surprisingly it was Keir who took over the initiative, asking her if she had seen the papers that day and what she thought of the present government policies. Politics

kept them going through most of the meal which
shortly followed, the discussion argumentative enough
to be interesting yet never allowed to get out of hand.
Keir's doing there too, Regan had to concede. He
refused to let heat creep into the proceedings, changing
the topic when it threatened to do so and setting her
off on a new tack.

'You've a good grasp,' he admitted with what she
considered quite infuriating condescension over dessert, 'but you might learn to keep a more open mind.'

'Sit on the fence, you mean?' she snorted. 'No,
thanks. There are quite enough doing that already!'

'Shall I take coffee through to the library, Miss
Regan?' asked Sullivan tactfully from the sidelines.
'And brandy for Mr Anderson, perhaps?'

'Make it two brandies,' she said. 'The best we have.
In fact, bring the bottle. Mr Anderson might want
more than one.'

Mr Anderson acknowledged the offer with a tilt of
his head, eyes faintly jeering. 'We'll see how it goes.'

It went very well. With the glow reaching down
inside her, Regan felt better equipped to get through
the rest of the evening. Keir watched her silently from
the opposite chair. He seemed to be waiting, as if in
recognition that she had something to ask. Whether
she could bring herself to do so was still in the lap of
the gods. What she needed was an opening.

In the end he provided that too, getting to his feet to
come across and draw her to hers, taking the glass from
her unresisting hand to place it on the table at the side
of her chair. His mouth was harder than she remembered it—or was that simply because hers refused
to yield to him? When he let her go it was without
undue reluctance, irony in his eyes.

'Just why did you invite me out here, Regan?' he
asked. 'It wasn't to take up where we left off, that's for
sure!'

She sought for the edge of the chair behind her with the back of her calves before answering, needing the support if only to stop her knees from trembling. 'In a way, it was,' she said. 'Only not that way. I don't want you kissing me, Keir. Not ever again. Do you hear?'

'You make it impossible not to.' His shrug revealed an almost insulting lack of concern. 'Supposing you tell me what it is you do want?'

'It's difficult,' she hedged, even now seeking a way out. 'To explain, I mean.'

'Try me.'

'All right.' She moved away from him first, her back turned to him as she poured herself another brandy. 'Could you use a large sum of money?'

The pause seemed to last an age but was probably only mere seconds. His voice when he answered was expressionless.

'How large?'

'Ten thousand.' She turned then to look at him, the glass clasped tautly in her hand. It was impossible to read what was going on in his mind. The grey eyes were impregnable. 'Enough?'

'That would depend,' he said levelly, 'on what you wanted me to do for it.'

'It's quite simple.' She took a deep breath, seeking the nerve to carry it through. When it came it sounded almost casual. 'I want you to marry me.'

CHAPTER TWO

WHATEVER Keir had been expecting, this had obviously not been it. For the space of several seconds he just stood there looking at her, mouth set in a line which made her nervous.

'Is this your idea of a joke?' he demanded harshly at length. 'Because if it is I'm going to be exercising my own brand of humour!'

'It's no joke.' Regan made a small gesture of appeal. 'Do you really think I'd be doing this if I had any other choice? If I don't have a husband by the time I'm twenty-five in five weeks' time I lose the house. It's as simple as that.'

'Simple?' His laugh was short. 'Sure it is! If it's only a husband you need there must be plenty of willing candidates.'

'Not for a marriage in name only,' she returned, and saw his expression change.

'I see. Or rather, I'm beginning to. Your father's idea, was it? Yes, it would have to be. A man of strong opinions but little perception, if he imagined you'd knuckle under to that kind of duress.'

'It isn't a case of knuckling under,' she retorted with control. 'I haven't found the man I'd want to marry yet, that's all.'

'So give up the house.'

'I won't do that either. He was wrong to set that kind of deadline. Given time I'll fulfil all his wishes, but only with a man I can love.'

His lip curled a fraction. 'That will be the day.' He paused then, expression enigmatic. 'How long would you expect the arrangement to last?'

'Until either of us wanted out for any reason.'

'And then?'

She shrugged, wishing she could feel as careless as she sounded. 'A quick annulment, what else? We'd be living apart anyway.'

'Me in Australia and you back here?'

'Of course. All I need from you is your name. On temporary loan, as you might say.'

'Not a lot,' he agreed. 'In fact, for ten thousand, very little at all.'

'Then you'll do it?'

'Why not?' It was his turn to shrug. 'I can think of harder ways of making a living. When would you want it to happen?'

'As soon as possible.' Now that she had it she could hardly believe it. It had been too easy—too lacking in any kind of moral hesitation. She said softly, 'You must need that money very badly.'

'Maybe.' His tone gave nothing away. 'Register office, of course?' It was a purely rhetorical question. 'I'll start making the arrangements first thing in the morning. At least we don't have to establish residency. If everything goes as it should we can be married on Thursday.'

Her voice sounded odd and far away. 'I'll pay all the expenses, naturally.'

'Oh, I think I can run to a licence and other odd fees. After all, it won't be a regular wedding, will it? No guests, or bridesmaids to buy presents for.'

'No.' Her throat felt dry. She gazed at him in silence for a moment, trying vainly to guess what he might be thinking. Mrs Keir Anderson. She must be mad to even contemplate it.

'It isn't too late,' he said, reading her own thoughts without apparent difficulty. 'You've a couple of days to change your mind.'

Oddly the offer served only to firm her resolution. 'I

shan't change my mind,' she assured him. 'You're all I've got to fall back on.'

'The last hope. Strange, isn't it,' he added on a dry note, 'how fate conspires? A day for new ventures, my horoscope promised me this morning. I'll take more note of the stars in future.' The pause was brief. 'In the meantime, I think I need that second brandy too.'

'Help yourself,' Regan told him, and moved away from the tray as he came towards her. Her limbs felt weak and shaky despite the brandy—or maybe partly because of it, she wasn't sure. She took a seat again, leaning her head back against the leather and trying to come to terms with her conscience.

'Supposing you fill me in on the whole story?' Keir suggested, resting a hip against the edge of the desk. 'Just to set the record straight, what exactly did your father's will say?'

She told him without emotion, holding nothing back. He looked at her narrowly when she had finished.

'If you don't come into full control of the estate until you're thirty, how do you expect to find ten thousand pounds to give me? I don't imagine the executors are likely to look too kindly on an ex-gratia payment of that particular nature.'

'You don't have to worry,' she came back stiffly. 'I have some money of my own left me by my grandmother. I'll have the draft ready by Thursday.'

'Isn't that going to leave you a little short for personal expenses?'

'Anything I need is advanced to me by Matt Swain, our family solicitor and also the sole executor—including all household expenses. As I'll be fulfilling the necessary conditions, they'll continue the same way. An income adequate to almost any life-style I care to live, he said. This is it.'

'Don't you find it lonely?' asked Keir.

'I have friends. And the Sullivans are always here. No, I don't find it lonely. I told you, I like my own company.'

'When it suits you to choose it,' he acknowledged. 'You're an odd mixture, Regan.'

'That needn't worry you either.' Her tone was short. 'If you've finished your brandy I really think you should be going. I could do with an early night.'

'Anything you say.' He drained the glass and put it down, lips twisted. 'Do we meet again before Thursday?'

'No.' That would be more, Regan thought, than she could bear. 'If I need to get in touch I'll phone the hotel.'

'I might not be in.'

'Then I'll leave a message for you to phone me back. Not that I think it will be necessary. What could go wrong?'

'The best laid plans of mice and men,' he quoted. 'I'd hate to lose out at the last minute.'

'You won't lose anything. Not even your freedom. You can be on your way by Thursday lunchtime if you arrange a morning appointment with the registrar.'

'What about a ring?' he asked.

'Oh, lord!' Regan closed her eyes momentarily, opening them again on the sight of his waiting face. 'No problem. I can use Grandmother's. She left me all her jewellery too. It might be a bit loose, but it will do.' She refused to consider what her grandmother might have thought about her using her wedding ring to such effect. If she was going through with this thing she had to do it wholesale. No looking for excuses. She said unsteadily, 'Please go, Keir. Sullivan will get your coat.'

He paused at the door, a hand on the knob and his features concealed. 'You're quite sure about everything?' he asked without turning his head. 'You don't want to change your mind?'

'No.' The firmness was as much for her own benefit as his. 'I don't want to change my mind. I'll see you on Thursday.'

She stayed where she was for a long time after he had gone, trying to keep any doubts at bay. She was doing what had to be done, no more, no less. It was the only way. She need tell no one outside of those who had to know of her change in circumstances. To all intents and purposes things would be just as they had been before, except that Cottam would be hers finally and irrevocably. For that alone it had to be worth it.

A warm front moving in from the south brought a swift melting of the snow on Wednesday night. By the next morning it had almost all cleared, leaving the roads gritty and wet and the trees dripping with moisture beneath a sky overcast and miserable.

Happy the bride the sun shines on, thought Regan with cynicism as she drove into town. Not that it really counted. A happy union was not her aim. In less than an hour she would have exchanged the name of O'Neil for Anderson, only few would be aware of it. Providing there was no intent to defraud, she was legally entitled to go on using her own name in general everyday transactions.

She had waited until the previous evening to tell John Sullivan of her decision. He had received the news with obvious distress mingled, it had to be admitted, with a certain relief. Now he could finish out his working days in the house he had loved and cherished for so many years. His home was safe. So was hers, she thought. Nothing could go wrong now. It was too late.

Keir was already in the register office waiting room when she arrived, wearing a dark blue shadow-striped suit with which she could find no fault. Her own choice had been for a plain grey coat and dress she had worn before and in which she felt comfortable. No point in dressing up, she had told herself firmly. She wasn't out to impress.

There was no smile, mocking or otherwise, on the strong, firm features this morning. He seemed to be taking the whole thing quite seriously. For ten thousand so he should, Regan reflected. She had the draft all ready in her handbag, and would be passing it over in due course.

'All set?' he asked, and she nodded.

'All set.'

In all her calculations, Regan had taken it for granted that the registrar, who had known her father, would be capable of keeping his own counsel on the subject of her marriage. What she had totally forgotten were the necessary witnesses, drawn as in all such cases from the registrar's staff. She knew both had recognised her the moment they entered the room, and realised with sinking heart that the news would take little time to filter through the whole town.

She was so busy wondering how the two might respond to a plea for silence that she scarcely heard a word of the proceedings, coming back to earth only when Mr Dailey spoke to her for the second time. She made the responses in a low but clear tone, listened to his own final declaration and received his congratulations with a sense of unreality. Mrs Anderson. Could that really be her? She didn't feel married—didn't feel anything very much. But it was hard fact.

Outside again it was Keir who was first to speak. 'So what next?'

Regan shook herself mentally. No use worrying about things now. It was over and done. If gossip spread then she would have to face it. People might not understand her reasons for this secret marriage, but if she just carried on as usual it would be little more than a nine-days' wonder. Her own immediate circle of friends were of more concern. Few of them were going to appreciate being left out in the cold. Robin Sayers in particular was going to find the whole affair a devastating kick in the teeth. Three times he had asked her to marry him and been gently turned aside with neither a definite yes or no. Looking back now, Regan supposed she had been subconsciously saving him as a final retreat. Robin was nice, and would have made a good if somewhat unexciting husband, but he deserved better than to be used as a means to an end.

'Well?' Keir sounded faintly impatient, as if eager to have this whole thing out of the way. 'Are we supposed to say goodbye right here in the street?'

'No, of course not.' She made herself meet the grey eyes, still unable to believe that this man was her husband. 'I've arranged to have lunch back at the house, then you can go on wherever you're going from there.'

'After I've been paid off?'

'If you like to put it that way.' She was determined that nothing he could say would get through to her now. 'We made a bargain, purely and simply.'

'So we did.' His tone lightened, almost deliberately. 'So let's go and eat.'

They travelled back to the house in convoy, Regan in the lead. She could see the dark head behind the wheel of the other car through her driving mirror whenever she glanced up. After leaving the town proper she stopped looking. In a little while he would be gone out of her life altogether. Until then she didn't want to consider anything but the moment.

Sullivan was at the door to greet them, his features composed into what he probably imagined was a blank mask. To Keir perhaps it was, but for Regan who knew him so well, there was pain in the ageing eyes. It was in an effort to counteract it that she put on her lightest, brightest voice, making believe she hadn't a trouble in the world now that Cottam was safe from the auctioneer's hammer.

Mrs Sullivan had gone all out to put on a special lunch regardless of circumstances, but Regan scarcely tasted what she ate of it. Keir seemed bound by no such restrictions on his appetite, trying everything with obvious appreciation.

'No champagne?' he asked at one point. 'Pity. I always thought it was mandatory at weddings.'

'Only when there's something to celebrate,' she returned. 'You could try a cigar with your coffee, if you like. Daddy left a whole stock properly stored. I don't think they'll have deteriorated.'

'I don't smoke,' he said. 'I never did, if you recall.'

'I thought you might have started.'

'Along with other vices?' He smiled, leaning back in his chair to survey the long, polished table. 'Whose idea was it to put me at the head?'

'Mine,' she said. 'It seemed the least I could do for the occasion.' Her glance at her watch was meant to be seen. 'I'll get your bank draft. You won't meet any trouble. It's all been arranged.'

Keir stayed where he was while she went to fetch it from her purse, taking the slip of paper from her with a total lack of expression. He didn't even bother to look at it, keeping his eyes fixed on her face as he tore it slowly and deliberately across the middle.

'I don't want your money,' he said. 'I've enough of my own.'

Regan could feel her heart beating up into her throat, and knew she had lost colour. Her voice when she found it sounded husky. 'Then what do you want?'

'You.' The inflection was hard and unyielding. 'I want you, Regan. I always did.'

In the sudden stillness the tick of the long case clock out in the hall seemed to fill the whole house. She stared at him in stunned dismay, scarcely knowing how to react.

'You can't be serious,' she whispered at last. 'We made a bargain, Keir!'

'We got married,' he came back. 'That gives me certain unassailable rights.'

'It does not!' There was a flush in her cheeks now, a spark in her eyes. 'Whatever you have in mind you can forget it, do you hear? That licence means nothing. It's just a piece of paper.'

'I'd like to hear you tell the authorities that. In their eyes it means a whole lot.'

'All right, then.' She sought for control, nails biting into the palms of her hands. 'So we're legally tied. That still doesn't give you any rights. We're in the twentieth century now, in case you hadn't noticed!'

'It's of no importance,' he said. 'Not to me. I came back here to find a girl who once made a fool of me, hoping to extract an appropriate penalty. You handed me my opportunity on a platter. Do you think I'm going to waste it?' His gaze travelled over her as she stood there, lingering with deliberation on the firm swell of her breasts beneath the thin grey wool, the curve of her hips. 'I often wondered if you could possibly look as good out of clothes as you do in them, and now I aim to find out. I'm going to have you, Regan. I'm going to take what should have been mine six years ago.'

'While I do what?' Her voice was stronger now, her lip curling. 'You must be mad if you think you're going to stay here! This is *my* house, *my* home. You don't have any place in it!'

'So try throwing me out,' he said. 'Better still, ask Sullivan to do it.'

Regan bit her lip, aware that he knew she would

drag in neither Sullivan or anyone else on a problem she herself had created. Physically incapable of doing as he suggested, she had to find a reasonable means of persuasion.

'If it's more money you want I can get it for you,' she forced through stiff lips. 'It might take a few days though.'

There was no weakening about the line of his mouth. 'I already told you, I'm not interested in your money. You're not going to buy me off, settle your mind to that.'

'I've certainly no intention of settling my mind to the alternative you're offering!'

'Not offering,' Keir responded. 'Demanding. And I can't think of a better time to start paying your dues than now.' He was pushing back his chair as he spoke, mouth slowly widening at her involuntary step backwards. 'You won't find it such an irksome duty, I can promise you. I've had six years to think about making love to you.'

'And plenty of other women to practise on, no doubt!'

There was irony in his voice. 'Not enough to make me forget my one and only true love. I laid it all at your feet, Regan. Now it's your turn. Come and show me your bedroom. I've waited too long already.'

The touch of his hand on her arm made her quiver. She shook it off fiercely, refusing to back off any further. 'There's no way I'm going to pay you anything but what we agreed. If you don't get out of here I'll send for the police!'

'And tell them what? That your new husband isn't quite the fool you took him for?' Keir shook his head, eyes mocking. 'Nothing they could do. It's a civil matter. You'd have to take me to court and get an injunction to make me stay away from you. That would mean telling the judge, and anyone else present, every sordid detail of what I'd done to you—and I don't intend raping you, so you'd have to persuade him there were other factors involved. You could say I beat you, but you'd still have to show your bruises. And there won't be any, I'll make sure of that.'

She was shaken despite herself. He had it all thought out, just as if he had planned the whole thing from the start. But he couldn't have, could he? He couldn't have known she would come up with such a proposition. As he had said just now, she had handed him the opportunity on a platter.

She tried another tack, hating herself for showing weakness yet unable to see any other way out. 'Keir, I said I was sorry for what I did all that time ago, and I am. I was eighteen and over-indulged, I know that. But I've changed. I wouldn't be that way now.'

'You haven't changed.' His voice was low but not soft. 'You still use people to suit your own ends. You're not wriggling out of it, Regan. I want you, and I want you *now*. We can go upstairs or we can make love right here. I don't mind. Sullivan might though if he comes in unexpectedly.'

Pride came to her rescue. Pride mingled with a hatred that seared. If he expected her to plead he would wait a long time. Not for anything would she give him that satisfaction. Submitting to his demands would tax her resources to the limit, but if that was the only way to get rid of him then she would force herself to go through with it. Given a total lack of response, he might realise that revenge was not after all so sweet.

She faced him squarely, lip curling in open contempt. 'All right, have it your own way. I'm not going to fight you, Keir. I wouldn't degrade myself!'

There was a flicker of something deep down in the grey of his eyes, but he didn't relent. 'So lead on,' he said.

None of the staff were in sight when they went out

to the hallway, much to Regan's relief. She took the stairs with the agility born of anger, knowing he was right behind her. Her bedroom lay off the open gallery, large and luxuriously furnished, the half-tester bed draped in silk. A faint current of cool air came into the room through the small casement window she had left open earlier. She went across to shut it, shivering a little despite the immediate blast of warmth from the built-in radiator as she turned up the control.

Behind her, she heard the door close softly, followed by the sound of a jacket being removed. She steeled herself to move back towards the bed, fingers plucking nervelessly at the tiny buttons fronting her dress. The sooner they got on with it the sooner it would be over.

It was only when she felt the third button go that pride finally deserted her, leaving her trembling with revulsion at her own actions. She couldn't go through with it. She *wouldn't* go through with it! There was no way he could make her.

Keir himself took the initiative out of her hands, coming across to turn her towards him. He had removed his tie and his shirt was opened almost down to the waist, revealing a chest covered in dark hair.

'You're not going to rob me of this pleasure either,' he said, moving her hands. 'I've dreamed of undressing you for too long.'

'I'm not a doll!' she flashed, striking his hand away from her.

'I know you're not.' He was smiling, his eyes lit by an expression she found infinitely disturbing. 'You're a real live adult woman, and you're going to react like one. Not a robot, darling. That wouldn't make me at all happy.'

He had known, she realised. He had guessed all along what she intended to do. She fought him desperately, aware that he had locked the door and that she wouldn't be screaming for Sullivan anyway.

She didn't win, of course. His strength was far greater than hers. He didn't even bother to struggle with her, simply picking her bodily up and tossing her on the bed, then following her down to seize her hands and pin them to the pillow behind her head as he found her mouth with his.

In all her life, Regan had never been kissed quite like that before. She felt the tremors run through her whole body, the heat spring deep in the pit of her stomach. His lips were never still, moving, caressing, forcing hers to yield and part, seeking deeper until they found a response she could no longer hold back.

She was aware of his hands moving over her, knowledgeable and experienced, of warmth and coolness on her skin. She no longer fought him because she had lost the desire to fight. Thought itself had receded to a far, far distance, leaving only sensation.

It was only when he paused that rationality returned to some extent. She was almost devoid of clothing, she realised dazedly, her body clad only in briefs and a wisp of a bra. Keir was still fully dressed, although his shirt had come away from his waistband—or been pulled away. Whether by him or by her, she couldn't be certain. These last few minutes had held the kind of abandonment she had never experienced before.

'You see?' he murmured. 'I told you it wouldn't be difficult. The times I've thought about this moment—having you under me, long and lovely, and ready. You're beautiful, Regan. As beautiful as I always imagined.' His hand was at her breast, his fingers moving with exquisite lightness and sensitivity, lips curving at the tiny moaning sound which broke involuntarily from her. 'You like that? It's only a beginning. I'm going to make you want me, the way I once wanted you. You're going to know what it's like to be played along until your whole body craves satisfaction. Remember how you used to let me touch you here—let me caress you just long enough to get me thoroughly roused, then push me away with all those wide-eyed protestations of innocence. I let you get away with it then because I believed you really were innocent.'

'I was.' Her eyes were closed, her throat aching with the effort to stop the sounds coming from it. 'I was!'

'Physically, maybe. Mentally, no way. You knew just what you were doing, how I felt about you—even what I was going to come to. You led me right into it, didn't you, my darling? Like a fly to the web!'

'Keir——' it was a whisper painfully forced '—don't be like this. What good will it do if you——' Her voice trailed away as she looked up into unrelenting eyes.

'If I take what I want?' he finished for her. 'If I use you the way you deserve to be used?' He shook his head, cruelty in the line of his mouth. 'I want more than just the bare satisfaction. I want to hear you beg. And before I'm through with you that's exactly what you will do—beg me to take you.'

'Never! I'll never do that!'

'Oh yes, you will. Believe me.' He sat up with a sudden decisive movement that took her by surprise, reaching for his shirt buttons while she lay there staring at him. 'There's tonight, and tomorrow, and all the other tomorrows to get through. How long do you think you can stand it?

She made to hit him with all her strength, a blind rage filling her, then gave a small cry of frustration as he promptly caught her hand.

'I'm no gentleman,' he said grimly. 'That's something else you should remember. I may have acquired a surface veneer, but underneath I'm the same uncouth character you once knew.'

'You were never uncouth,' she protested suddenly chagrined. 'I never called you that!'

'You called me rustic, which meant the same thing. Just take warning, Regan. You'll get back as good as you give. I may vary the retaliation, but the result will be the same.'

'Swine!' she whispered, and saw the smile she hated cross his lips.

'Only so far. You'd better get dressed—unless you plan on staying in bed for the rest of the day.' He bent to pick up the dress and tights he had dropped at the side of the bed, viewing the latter with masculine distaste. 'The worst invention of the century! What happened to stockings and suspenders?'

She made no answer, sliding off the far side of the bed to reach for the robe draped across the foot and wrap it around her. Her hair had come loose from its smooth French pleat to swing down about her face in heavy, reddish gold waves, hiding her features from his gaze. She couldn't even begin to think straight yet.

'I want you out of here,' she said.

'I'm your husband,' Keir came back flatly, 'and I'm staying. The rest of my things are in the car. I'll go and fetch them in.' He glanced back at her when he reached the door, adjusting the fit of his jacket with a shrugging movement of broad shoulders. 'Don't go away.'

There was nowhere to go, she acknowledged. Nowhere to go, and no one she could turn to. She had to face this thing alone.

CHAPTER THREE

REGAN was in the bathroom with the door locked and bolted when Keir returned. For a wild moment after he had left her, she had actually contemplated slipping down after him and locking the outer doors too, but common sense had pointed out the futility of any such action. The kind of man Keir Anderson was proving to be would hardly think twice about breaking a window to gain re-entry to the house, and what would the staff make of that? She could face any degradation but that of having others know what she had got herself into.

He was sitting waiting for her in one of the two easy chairs when she finally emerged. A leather suitcase stood over by the door.

'I unpacked for myself,' he said. 'You might get somebody to stick that away somewhere until I need it again.'

'Which will be when?' she asked, and saw his shoulders lift.

'That rather depends.'

'I'm sure it does.' She made no effort to keep the contempt from her voice. 'Why settle for ten thousand when there's obviously so much more to be had!'

Whatever he was thinking, Keir remained outwardly unmoved. 'If it comforts you to think that, go right ahead. In the meantime, I wouldn't mind taking a shower. I gather that's what you've been doing all this time I've been sitting out here?'

'I needed to wash the feel of your hands off me,' she retorted. 'It took a lot of water!'

This time he definitely looked amused. 'You're going

35

to be needing an awful lot more if that's the case.' He got to his feet, shaking his head in response to her change of expression. 'Not now. Later. Even honeymooners take time off to recuperate. We'll spend the rest of the day quietly and companionably—getting to know one another, it's called. You can tell me all about what you've been doing with yourself this last six years.'

'I wouldn't tell you the time of day!'

'I wouldn't need to ask you,' he came back dryly. 'There's a surfeit of clocks around this place.' His tone altered, taking on a subtly harder note. 'Reconcile yourself to it, Regan. You're going to give me everything I want in the end. I don't care how long it takes.'

She watched him in the bathroom without answering. There was nothing to say, nothing he might listen to. He had closed his mind against any plea of hers a long, long time ago.

On impulse she went to open doors in the long wall fitting until she found what she was looking for. Two suits, the tweed jacket he had worn that first time in the café, a couple of pairs of slacks and, in the shelf fitting, several neatly folded shirts and some underwear. Not a lot, but then there wouldn't be, would there? Men notoriously travelled light.

She fingered materials and looked at labels, not a lot wiser afterwards as they were all of Australian origin. Well tailored, but perhaps good tailoring came cheaper over there anyway. There was nothing in any of the pockets to enlighten her any further. Keir's Australian background remained an enigma.

She should take the opportunity to dress while he was busy showering, she realised suddenly. Hurriedly she picked out a finely knitted skirt and top of amber bouclé, and put them on over clean underwear. For a brief moment her hand actually hesitated over the box of new tights in her drawer before taking out a pair and pulling them resolutely up her legs. Stockings and suspenders were fine on occasion, but this certainly wasn't one of them. She would do nothing to make herself attractive to Keir.

He was wearing a towel draped casually about lean hips when he opened the door some moments later. With no trace of selfconsciousness, he moved across the room to take fresh briefs from the shelf in the wardrobe, just as casually dropping the towel in order to pull them into place. He had his back to her, and was naked for mere seconds, but Regan felt the colour flood her cheeks. She couldn't look away, aware of the deep tanned smoothness of his back throwing into sharp relief the narrow strip of contrast, the muscular thighs. Her whole chest felt tight, the thud of her heart loud in her ears. For a blind moment she knew what it was to want something against which all her sensibilities fought.

He turned before she could move, brows lifting sardonically as he registered her expression.

'You never saw a man dress before?'

'I never had a man perform for me before,' she responded scathingly, recovering her poise with an effort. 'You did that purposely. Why? Were you hoping I might be fired with lust by the very sight of your manly physique?'

His laugh held derision. 'The time to worry about that is when I start taking things off, not putting them on! You're safe enough for the moment.'

'What kind of a man are you?' Despite all she could do to control it, there was a shake in her voice. 'There has to be something radically wrong with anyone who'd spend six years planning this kind of revenge!'

'I didn't plan anything.' His own voice was perfectly level. 'Until the moment I saw you crossing High Street the other day I had no real intention of even looking you up.'

She started at him nonplussed. 'You said——'

'I know what I said.' His shrug was dismissive. 'I'm not going to pretend I haven't thought about you at times—imagined what it would be like to have you where I wanted you—but that's about it. That offer of yours was a gift from the gods. I accepted it in the same spirit.'

'The devil would be more likely,' Regan retorted with feeling. 'At least you'll feel at home when you finally get there!'

'Ten to one I'll be meeting a lot of old friends,' he agreed, tucking his shirt into the waistband of his slacks. 'Stop being childish Regan. You're not going to reach me by a dint of name-calling.'

She drew in a steadying breath as he reached for a light fawn sweater and pulled it over his head, waiting for his head to emerge before saying tautly, 'Just how long do you intend keeping this up?'

'As long as it takes,' came the unmoved response. 'I already told you that.'

'And then?'

'You mean when I'm satisfied?' His glance held mockery. 'You admit there's a chance?'

Regan stood her ground resolutely. 'I admit nothing. Just answer the question.'

'We'll just have to wait and see, won't we? How long depends entirely on you.'

She gave up then, acknowledging the futility in banging one's head against a brick wall. Keir was determined to make her eat humble pie, and she was equally determined not to. There had to be some other way of getting him out of her home, out of her life. She simply had to find it.

Whatever the solution might be it was going to be far from simple, she had to admit to herself before the day was through. While making no attempt to take any authority over the household out of her hands, he had managed to convey the impression of a permanent fixture sufficiently well to convince even her that persuasion, in any form, was not going to be the answer. Physical force seemed the only reasonable alternative, yet who in the household was capable of applying it? Apart from Barlow, the gardener, Sullivan was the only other man around, and one could hardly ask or expect a sixty-three-year-old man to tackle another less than half his age. What it needed was someone as young and as fit and loaded with incentive, she reasoned. But who? The only candidate to spring to mind was Robin Sayers, and he hardly fitted the bill.

Sullivan cornered her in the library just before dinner, his uncertainty plain to see.

'I'm perhaps speaking out of turn, Miss Regan,' he said with some diffidence, 'but it was understood Mr Anderson would be leaving after lunch. Should a room be made ready for him?'

Regan replaced the book she had been riffling through on the shelf before answering, not looking at the man she had known all her life. It had to be said because there was no way round it, but she knew how it was going to sound.

'Another room won't be needed,' she stated with all the coolness she could muster. 'Mr Anderson will be sharing mine.'

'But he isn't—you don't——' he broke off confusedly, recollecting his position. 'I beg your pardon, I must have misunderstood.'

'That's all right.' There was little else she could say. Telling Sullivan the truth would serve no purpose other than to upset him further. He would have to believe she had changed her mind about this marriage of hers, that was all. She must already have lost some of his respect by contracting it in the first place; a little more wasn't going to make any great difference.

Keir chose that moment to put his head round the door, his expression revealing little change when he saw the two of them together.

'There you are,' he said. 'I was wondering where you'd got to.' He came farther into the room, his glance resting on Sullivan as the latter began moving in the direction of the door. 'I was just about to suggest a drink before dinner. Why don't you join us?'

Under other circumstances, Regan might have felt moved to inward laughter at the affronted drawing up of the spare frame. Right now she could only agree with the reason for it. Keir was taking things too far—and purposely.

'Sullivan doesn't drink,' she said coldly before he could find any answer himself. 'We'll eat as soon as you're ready,' she added on a more normal note for the older man's benefit.

Keir eyed her with unconcealed amusement as the door closed firmly. 'Lesson number one?'

'Deliberate ignorance doesn't yield to corrective teaching,' she returned with contempt. 'Don't bother trying to sway Sullivan to your "We're all brothers together" policies. He's not interested in your kind of equality.'

'Being as hidebound in his way as you are in yours,' he observed pleasantly, pouring sherry. 'Not a lot I can do about our Mr Sullivan. He's too set in his habits.' He picked up the glass and held it out to her, mouth sardonic. 'You're still young enough to learn new ones.'

'Something else you're going to teach me?' she asked silkily, making no attempt to take the glass from him. 'I didn't ask for a drink, thanks.'

'I know you didn't ask, but as I've poured it anyway you can do me the courtesy of taking a token sip.' There was a dangerous gleam in the grey eyes. 'Here.'

If it hadn't been for the suspicion that he almost wanted her to refuse, Regan might have considered it. Under the circumstances, she made herself shrug as if it failed to matter either way and took the glass, lifting it to her lips in an exaggerated salutation to drain the contents at one swallow.

'I don't make token gestures,' she said. 'Only meaningful ones.' She was holding out the glass as she spoke. 'You may as well have this back.'

Keir took it from her, putting his own down at the same time. In the act of turning away, she found herself caught and held by the arm which had snaked about her waist from the rear, felt him close in behind her so that she couldn't move.

'I've a feeling,' he said softly in her ear, 'that you and I are going to have to come to more than one kind of understanding before we're through, Madame Anderson!'

She was stiff and unyielding in his grasp, afraid to relax any part of her body against him. 'Don't call me that!' she got out between her teeth.

'Why not? It's what you are. Common Mrs wouldn't be good enough for you, sweetheart.' His free hand slid up and under her arm, finding her breast in a caress that made her skin tingle, fingers registering her immediate and totally involuntary response. 'Just to keep you ticking over,' he murmured, and gave her a light slap on the behind as he let her go. 'Now we both know where we stand.'

Dinner was a silent meal. Facing Keir down the length of the mahogany table, Regan wondered how any man could change so radically. The younger Keir had been assertive to a point, perhaps, but there had been no hardness about him. There had to be causes other than what had passed between them to make him that way, she reasoned. She was simply bearing the cumulative brunt.

'I think in future we'll both sit at the same end of the table,' he remarked dryly half way through dessert. 'This baronial hall effect is quite ridiculous.'

Regan had been thinking the same thing herself up until the moment he spoke, but her immediate reaction was a total change of mind.

'I prefer it this way,' she responded coolly.

'Because it's traditional?' His tone was light, but with an underlying note not to be ignored. 'So we'll start a new one.' His glance moved to the man who had just brought in the coffee. 'You might see to that, Sullivan.'

Meeting the latter's swift, questioning look, Regan forced herself to appear unconcerned. Whatever Sullivan might think of her it had to be better than if he knew the truth. Whether he followed Keir's orders or not remained to be seen.

Avoiding the intimacy of the library after the meal was over, she made for the sitting room, switching on the television and setting herself determinedly down in front of it with the firm intention of not uttering one word unless she was forced. Let Keir make his own entertainment!

It wasn't until he asked her on an amused note if she particularly liked stand-up comedians that she even realised what she was watching so assiduously. Fortunately the act finished at that moment, and the show's star appeared on screen to sing his next number, enabling her to make out that this was what she had been waiting for.

'He still has what it takes,' she said stoutly, 'regardless of how long he's been going.'

'Like nerve?' came the dry suggestion. 'There should be a mandatory retirement age for singers. Technique can't overcome all deterioration, as I'm sure you must admit.'

'Sinatra still draws them in', she defended, stifling the part of her which had to agree. 'People wouldn't pay all that money to see him if he'd lost it all.'

'They pay to see a legend. Being truly loyal fans

they're not going to kick their idol in the teeth for want of youthful strength. He gave it to them in the past, now it's their turn.'

Regan was silent for a long moment, realising the uselessness of argument. 'You're so convinced you have to be right,' she said at last with scorn.

'Only where the conclusion is obvious.'

Keir was sitting at ease in a nearby chair, his whole attitude so casually relaxed she knew a sudden blinding desire to do something—anything—to disrupt that equanimity. But what? She could think of nothing that might get through to him. He was as impregnable as a Sherman tank—and twice as dangerous.

'Penny for them,' he said now, watching her face. 'Or are they worth more than that?'

'Where you're concerned, they're not worth anything,' she retorted, not bothering to keep the contempt out of her voice. 'You might think you're all sorts of a big man, but in my book you're nothing, Keir. Nothing at all!'

There was no reaction that she could see in the lean, dark features. He just kept right on looking at her in the same steady fashion. When he did speak it was almost conversationally.

'If I thought putting you across my knee might do you any real good I'd give myself the pleasure. As it is, it would only be an indulgence. There's only one place you're going to learn to respect me, Regan, and that's flat on your back!' His move to rise was slow and measured. 'An early night seems indicated. Our wedding night, in case you'd forgotten.'

She eyed him with chin held high, making no attempt to get up. 'I'm not ready to go yet, so what are you going to do about that?'

'So I'll carry you,' he said, and suited his actions to his words, bending to scoop her bodily from the chair. 'Who said romance was dead!'

Held against the broad, hard chest, Regan found she could neither struggle free nor make any impression with her clenched fist. The thought of what was to come brought a desperation not wholly attributable to rejection, the memory of how it had been earlier too fresh in her mind for total disregard. To be taken against her will was one thing, to be persuaded to give regardless of it quite another. She had to fight him, and keep on fighting him, futile or not.

Keir's immediate answer was to pin her free arm down to her side with hard fingers, his other arm curved under her knees in a way which made any kind of kicking practically impossible.

'You're going to give Sullivan a bad night if he sees you struggling,' he observed, making his way towards the door. 'You wouldn't want him to think you were unhappy in your choice of a husband, would you? After all, nobody pushed you into it.'

Regan had already thought of that possibility herself, and knew she had little choice. She let the tension drain from her limbs, said low-toned, 'All right, put me down. I'll walk.'

'No way.' He had the door open; now he carried her through. 'I've no intention of having to chase you half-way through the house. You know it better than I do. I'll put you down when we reach that bed of yours.' His mouth curved ironically. 'I mean "of ours". And save your breath—you're going to need it.'

He was fit, she had to concede him that. By the time they reached the bedroom he was breathing very little faster himself, and there was no sign of sagging in his hold.

Dropped on the bed, she lay there motionless looking up at him, searching for even the faintest hint of softening in his expression. There was none. If anything, the grey eyes were harder than they had been before—or was it just her growing agitation which made them seem so? She watched his hands as he peeled off his sweater and started to unfasten his shirt, long, lean and deeply tanned; suggestive of strength even in so measured a movement. A shudder ran through her—not totally unpleasant in its connotations. In a few moments those hands would be holding her, moving over her body, seeking a response she knew was going to be difficult to withhold in spite of everything she felt. Keir knew too much about women, about lovemaking: where to touch, where to linger, how to undermine every last defence until she abandoned all resistance. It had been like that this afternoon; it would be like that again tonight. There was no way of stopping him.

This time he undressed her totally, removing each garment with practised ease before sliding down at her side to take her in his arms. His lips were unexpectedly tender on hers, a featherlike brushing motion which brought every sense in her achingly alive, the touch of his tongue at the corner of her mouth like fire and ice at one and the same time. She felt her body move against him, and knew then that it was already too late. She wanted this to happen, wanted it with a need that transcended all other influences. Tomorrow could take care of itself. Tonight there was only Keir, the man she had married—the only man who had ever made her feel the way she did at this moment.

There was finesse as well as skill in his handling of her during the timeless period following: a strategy designed to bring her within a hairsbreadth of fulfilment and hold her there in quivering anticipation. It was then, looking down into her wild, abandoned eyes, that he brought the words out softly.

'Say it, Regan. I want to hear you say it.'

Sanity returned with all the impact of a douche of cold water in the face, stiffening her whole body in his arms. The descent from overwhelming desire to vehement rejection was accomplished in seconds, one arm coming up across his throat with a fierceness that could have snapped his neck had he not been ready for it.

'Bastard!' she choked. 'You lousy, rotten bastard!'

Close as he had brought her to total submission, he was still in control of himself, the latter fact evidenced by the slow, mocking curve of his lips. 'Such language from a high-born lady! I should wash your mouth out.'

He was capable of that too, she knew that now. He was capable of anything he deemed necessary to her subjugation. It made little difference to her right then. Her voice sounded harsh in her ears.

'Get away from me!'

His move to obey the injunction took her by surprise, holding her frozen into stillness as he pushed himself upright. The glance he ran down the length of her body held deliberation.

'It isn't over yet, not by any means. I hope you don't need a lot of sleep.'

Regan rolled over as he got up, pulling the cover across her and burying her face in the pillow. She heard him move across the room, the opening of a door and a moment later the rushing sound of the shower turned on at full blast. Only when the door was closed again between them did she make any attempt to lift her head, seeing the familiar room through a blur of angry tears. Everything that had happened between them had been planned, right down to the last fine detail. Keir had controlled her the way he might control a puppet. But only up to a point, she reminded herself forcibly. She had not been so far gone as to do as he wanted. And she never would be, no matter what manner of persuasion he used. On that she was determined.

She was sufficiently in control of herself by the time he emerged from the bathroom to have pulled on a robe and cleared away the garments he had taken from her. His own things she had left where they were on the floor. He was wearing the white towelling bath-robe she sometimes used herself, and which originally had been her father's, the length mid-thigh on him where on her it reached the knees. His hair was damp and curling slightly at the ends, lending a subtle dif-ference to the strong, hard features. More the old Keir than the new, she caught herself thinking, and stifled the sudden flood of longing with harsh intent. The old Keir was gone for good. That was something she had to face. This man looking back at her now was totally devoid of any kind of mercy.

'Ready for bed?' he asked. 'That's good.'

'I'd like to use the shower too,' she retorted, trying for a level note. 'Preferably with Lysol in it!'

'Try carbolic,' came the unmoved reply. 'I never could stand the smell.' Grey eyes mocked her. 'Don't take too long about it or I'll be in to fetch you out. The night's only just got started.'

Regan passed him without a word, steeling herself not to flinch from his close proximity. With the bath-room door closed and locked she felt safe enough to relax a little, viewing her face in the bronzed wall mirror with a sense of surprise that she could look so untouched by all that had taken place. Whether she would still look as fresh by morning was another matter. Keir had not been joking. He intended making love to her again. It wasn't going to be easy to remain inviolate to his kind of calculated assault, but she would do it if it killed her!

She stayed as long as she dared under the shower, letting the warmth wash over her. Only when she finally forced herself to get out did she realise that her night things were back in the bedroom, leaving her with no alternative but to go and fetch them.

Keir was already in bed when she went out, lying on his back with his head supported by clasped hands. He made no move to look at her as she crossed the room to take a clean nightdress from a drawer.

Safely back in the bathroom again, Regan slipped off the wrap and pulled on the cotton garment chosen deliberately for its lack of sensuality. High-necked and short-sleeved, it was one she had never used before yet never got around to throwing out. A present from Great-Aunt Daphne, she remembered now. How long was it since she had seen her? She supposed she should really make more effort to keep in touch with her only surviving relative.

Given the total cover-up of the nightdress, the wrap was superfluous, but she put it on again anyway, belting it about her slim waist with fingers that trembled a little in spite of her resolve. There was no further excuse to linger. She had to go out there. She could attempt to find another bed, of course, but she doubted if Keir was going to let her do that. He would not be asleep, of that one could be certain. He would be waiting for her.

He was still in the same position, she found, but his eyes were closed, his breathing deep and even. Gazing at him from the foot of the bed, she wondered how any man so physically attractive could harbour the kind of mind he harboured. Malice and cruelty were only two of the elements involved in this campaign of his.

He spoke without opening his eyes, tone level. 'Are you coming to bed, or do I fetch you?'

All in all, Regan decided with reluctance, it would be better to retain some form of initiative, spurious or not. She moved slowly round the bottom post, slipping off her wrap as she went, and put out a hand to click the switch controlling both bedside lights before sliding between the sheets. Lying rigidly on her own side of the mattress, she waited for whatever was due to come her way, hearing the beat of her heart like thunder through her head.

It was a moment or two before Keir made a move,

rolling on to his side with his back to her and space between them.

'Relax,' he said. 'I've decided to give us both a respite. There's time enough.'

'Losing heart?' she taunted without stopping to think about it, and could have bitten off her tongue the moment she had said it.

The reply came soft. 'That I can control. If I make love to you again tonight I'm not sure I can stop myself from taking you regardless, and I don't intend letting you off the hook that easily. Go to sleep, Regan.'

She lay silently gazing into the darkness, aware of a sense of almost anticlimax. But it wasn't finished by any means; Keir had said as much. Tomorrow it would all begin again. She had a weapon of sorts to use against him now, it was true, but it was double-edged. Would she be prepared to employ it?

CHAPTER FOUR

KEIR was gone from the bed when she awoke. Had it not been for the indentation left by his head in the pillow beside her, she might have believed the whole affair nothing but a bad dream.

The bedside clock said seven-forty-five—early by her standards but apparently not by Keir's. The bathroom door stood wide open, with no sound from within. If he had gone down expecting breakfast he was going to be unlucky. Regan usually had a tray brought to her room at eight-thirty. Having received no orders to the contrary, Sullivan would probably have taken it that the same arrangement would apply for two.

Thinking about the previous night brought an odd mixture of emotions. If she had gone along with what Keir was demanding of her they might have been lying here together right now in a different kind of closeness. She caught herself up there, sensing something deep within her that could not be allowed to gain an upper hand. All Keir really wanted was her degradation, and he wasn't going to have it. There was no way she was ever going to plead with him to finish what he had started.

He came back on the half hour, using an elbow to push the door open due to the loaded tray he carried in his hands.

'I met Sullivan on his way up with this little lot,' he said. 'Thought I'd save him the trouble. I understand the toast and marmalade are for you, and the ham and eggs for me. Good thinking on his part. I like to start the day on a full stomach.'

Regan sat up in the bed as he brought the tray across

to set it down on the swivel table she had pulled out ready from the panelling at the side of the bed.

'Nifty arrangement,' he commented. 'One of those at my side too?'

'It's a double bed,' she returned shortly. 'Naturally there are two.'

'Handy when you have guests,' he murmured, and drew a bitter glance.

'You're the only man I ever shared this bed with, and that wasn't exactly by choice!'

Grey eyes met green with an implacable expression. 'You know what I want.'

'I know what you say you want.' Her tone was biting. 'I think that's only a part of it!'

Keir was moving even while she was still speaking, taking hold of the covered plate holding his own breakfast to carry it round to the other side of the bed. 'Tell me more,' he said, pulling out the table. 'I can listen while I eat.'

He turned his back to her when he sat down on the edge of the bed to pick up the knife and fork. Perhaps fortunately, her own butter knife was too blunt an instrument to make any impression on the muscular breadth, but for a fierce fleeting moment the desire was right there in her. Close contact with a man of his nature heightened all the emotions, not just the one. She wanted to hurt him physically.

'You're after all this, aren't you?' she said on a contemptuous note. 'Get me to the point where I can't say no to you and it all falls into your lap!'

'It's quite a thought,' he admitted, not bothering to turn his head. 'Master of Cottam Manor! I'll have to work a little harder on you.'

Regan pushed away her own table in sudden dry-throated distaste. 'Why don't you just go away?' she demanded thickly. 'You're not going to win, Keir. I won't let you win!'

'We'll see.' He sounded unmoved.

She remained silent because there was nothing else to say, pouring fresh coffee with a hand that had a definite shake to it. There was no getting through to him—no way of bringing pressure to bear. He could treat her as he saw fit and little enough she could do about it. There was no one to complain to—at least, no one she could bear to complain to. So far as outsiders were concerned, everything had to appear normal. She couldn't take it if anyone ever found out just how far she had been taken for a ride.

'Where did you go?' she asked at length in an attempt to regain some initiative. 'This morning, I mean.'

'Running,' he said. 'Two miles cross-country. Back home I do an hour's jogging first thing before it gets too hot. Wakes me up for the day.' He laid down the knife and fork with an air of satisfaction, wiping his mouth on the napkin. 'That was excellent. Can't say I'm all that keen on eating up here, though.'

'It saves time for the staff.'

'Hardly a valid reason.' He had a shoulder resting against the bedpost, one knee lifted comfortably on top of the cover. 'What you really mean is you can't get yourself out of bed early enough to make the effort worthwhile.'

He was too near the mark for comfort. Early rising was only compatible when there was something to get up for.

'I don't eat enough at breakfast to merit the breakfast room,' she defended, feeling the need.

'Well, you should. It's vital to good health.' He paused and shrugged. 'Anyway, I do, so we'll eat downstairs tomorrow morning. For now, you might start thinking about getting up. There are things I'd like to do today.'

About to ask what, Regan was forestalled by the

bleep of the telephone. Keir made no move as she put out a hand to lift the receiver.

The voice on the other end of the line was only too familiar, the tone alight with excited curiosity: 'Regan, you dark horse! I only heard last night! I'll never forgive you for not telling me—me, of all people! You know I'd never have breathed a word if that's what you wanted!'

Regan's knuckles showed white where they gripped the receiver, regaining colour as she resignedly accepted the inevitable. The grapevine had been at work; by now the whole town probably knew. She had to face it out the best way she could.

'Sorry, Fiona,' she said on a penitent note. 'We decided not to tell anyone.' She was conscious of Keir's presence, knowing he was listening to the conversation. 'Look, I can't talk now. Why don't I ring you back in half an hour or so?'

'You mean you're still in bed?' The pause itself was full of innuendo, the chuckle which followed it even more so. 'Darling, it's gone nine! That must be some man you married! Who is he anyway? All I got was his name—Anderson, isn't it? *Mrs* Anderson. I just can't believe that's you, Regan! Are you still there?'

"I'm here.' Regan forced herself to say it, too well aware that Fiona Huntley was one person unlikely to have forgotten any details of past indiscretions—her own or anyone else's. 'You'll probably know him when you see him, although it was a long time ago.'

'You mean I've actually met him before?' The curiosity had acquired a new high. 'When? I don't remember anybody called Anderson. Only——' This time the pause was longer, the sound of her breathing clearly audible down the line. When she did speak again her voice held a totally new note. 'Regan, you don't mean—not *Keir* Anderson?'

'The same.' Keir had to have heard his name spoken

in such ringing tones of disbelief. She kept her face turned resolutely front. 'He came back to Cottam a few days ago.'

'But, *darling*, how romantic!' Fiona sounded as if she really meant it; there was a more than even chance that she did. 'Keir Anderson. Yes, I do remember him. Tall and dark, and absolutely devastating! I never could understand how you came to let him get away in the first place!'

That was an outright lie to start with, Regan reflected dryly. Fiona had known exactly how—and why. As her closest friend the other girl had been privy to all her secrets. Keir had been no exception. She had told Fiona everything that had passed between them. At twenty-four, she could look back on that fact with shame; at eighteen it had all been part and parcel of the excitement. Fortunately she wasn't called upon to comment as Fiona carried straight on:

'You know what I'm going to do? I'm going to throw a party for the two of you! Let's make it tonight. I can't think of anybody likely to be unavailable when they hear the news!'

'Tonight?' Regan sat up straighter, her mind seeking excuses—any excuses. 'Fiona, that's ridiculous! You can't possibly——'

'Who can't? I've done it before. I rise to a challenge, you know that. Compared with some things I've tackled, tonight's little event will be a doddle, believe me!' Her tone brooked no refusal. 'It has to be tonight—unless you want me over there right now? The chuckle came again, infectious in quality. 'I just can't wait to see you both!'

Regan tried again, knowing even as she did so how futile an effort it was. 'We may not be able to manage it tonight.'

'Why not? You're obviously not going away on honeymoon, and you can't spend every minute in bed.'

Fiona laughed. 'I'll tell you what. If you don't turn up, we'll all come to you!'

She wasn't joking; Regan was too well aware of that. What Fiona wanted she made certain she got. 'All right,' she said flatly. 'We'll be there.'

Keir glanced at her as she replaced the receiver, assessing her expression with lifted brows. 'Mind telling me just where it is we're supposed to be tonight?'

'Not supposed,' she said. 'We have to go. If we don't turn up, Fiona's threatening to bring everybody over here instead. She'd do it too.'

'Fiona?'

'Huntley. I don't think——'

'I remember her.' The statement was dry. 'Cute little brunette. Father in merchant banking. Has an uncle in light engineering. I was in his employment for a couple of years after I left the Poly.'

Regan had forgotten that detail but doubted if Fiona had. The 'cute brunette' was going to enjoy herself tonight.

'I gathered my name wasn't exactly unknown to her,' Keir added 'How much does she know about our previous relationship?'

'Everything.' The word came out with quite deliberate intent to wound. 'I told her everything!'

'A regular little blabbermouth, weren't you?' He said it evenly enough, but there was no humour in his expression. 'Good thing I didn't realise it at the time.'

'Why?' she asked on a faintly derisory note. 'What would you have done?'

'Probably half killed you—as I would now if I caught you confiding in her again.' He shot out a sudden hand to gather up the front of her nightdress in a taut grip, pulling her half clear of the bedclothes as he drew her towards him. His eyes were steely. 'Whatever happens between two people is their business and no one else's. Understand?'

His fingers were hard where they touched her, the pulled material tight under her armpits. Held only bare inches away from the grimly set mouth, Regan could find little spirit to answer him with.

'I was eighteen,' she appealed. 'Do you think I haven't learned anything since then?'

'Not a great deal,' he said. 'But you're doing it now.'

The kiss was ruthless, forcing her lips back against her teeth and bringing the salt taste of blood into her mouth. She took it because she had no choice, knowing she had asked for it.

The steel still lingered in his eyes when he lifted his head. 'That's a working example of what it could be like, given the incentive. Don't underestimate me, Regan.'

There was little chance of that, she thought painfully. Not any more. 'You made your point,' she said on a subdued note. 'Do you mind if I get up now?'

He let go of her at once. 'Go right ahead.'

She was pulling on her wrap when he added unexpectedly, 'I arranged to meet Jake Carter for a lunchtime drink today. Want to come along?'

About to refuse, Regan paused in resignation, acknowledging the futility of trying to avoid the issue any further. She had to meet Keir's friends some time, just as he had to meet hers tonight. At least for her it would only be the one person. She could surely cope with that.

'Why not?' she said. 'I've nothing much else to do. What time are you seeing him?'

'Twelve-thirty at the George. Just a pub lunch, so mink and pearls aren't essential.'

'That's fortunate,' she came back with sarcasm. 'I don't possess a mink, and my mother's jewellery is lodged at the bank. Would an ordinary sheepskin offend your sense of propriety too much?'

There was a certain wry quality to the movement of

his head. 'So it was a rotten crack. Put it down to my own lack of good taste.'

Regan had no answer to that; Keir had taken the wind out of her sails. She said instead, 'When did you make this arrangement with Jake?'

'Day before yesterday,' he admitted. He met her eyes steadily. 'Yes, I told him the news. I didn't want him to hear it casually.'

'The way my friends heard it?'

'That was entirely your own doing. You were the one who wanted secrecy.'

She was hardly able to argue with that. Regan made herself shrug and turn away as if the whole subject had lost point.

She didn't bother locking the bathroom door. There was little point in that either. Turning on the shower, she stripped off her nightdress, then stood for a moment trying to straighten things out in her mind. How long would it be before Keir tired of this cat and mouse game he had formulated it was hard to tell, though judging by last night's lack of follow-up he was already finding it something of a strain. As his wife by her own choice she had little grounds for complaint if and when he did tire of it. He wouldn't have to use force; he had already taught her that much about herself. In his arms she was a different person, forgetful of everything but what he was doing to her.

Wanton, she thought in swift self-abasement, but she knew it wasn't true. No one but Keir had ever managed to undermine her control this way. With him the whole act of lovemaking was an art, and he the master of it. Hate him or not, it made little difference to the way he could make her respond to him. If she were honest with herself she had to admit there was a very good chance that she might be the first to break.

And what then? she wondered, adjusting the hot water control with an unsteady hand. Could two people as far apart emotionally as they were ever hope to live together in harmony?

The answer had to be no.

The George was right in the centre of town, a mock-Tudor fronted building under a preservation order because two of its walls dated back to the seventeenth century. Jake greeted them in the lounge bar, surprising Regan who had expected to find him knocking back a pint in the saloon. Pure arrogance on her part, she reflected ruefully. It was high time she started throwing out that kind of preconception.

Seeing him now, she had a vague recollection of the Jake Carter of six years ago. Smaller in build than Keir, he had one of the most cheerfully appealing faces she had ever seen on a man, his eyes glinting with unconcealed speculation as he looked across the corner table at them both.

'Didn't manage to keep it quiet for very long, did you?' he observed. 'I've had at least six people ask me if I heard about the two of you getting married so suddenly. I kept mum, of course.'

'Thanks.' Regan tried hard to keep any irony from her voice. 'I suppose it was a forlorn hope to start with.'

'For somebody like you it was. I could get married any day of the week and nobody any wiser!'

'Does that mean you're not?' she asked in an attempt to sidetrack the conversation. 'Married, I mean.'

'Haven't found the right one yet,' he admitted without undue concern. 'Not like some.' The last with a grin in Keir's direction. 'Always knew what he wanted, even if it meant coming all the way back from Australia to get it!' He paused, shaking his head. 'You know, I still can't take it in. Only last Sunday when you got into town, and now this!' His eyes were back on Regan's face, expression bemused. 'Congratulations anyway.'

'You're supposed to say that to me,' put in Keir on a dry note.

'Ladies first, I was always taught,' came the un-abashed response. More soberly Jake added, 'All the best to you both, and I really mean that.'

Up until this moment Regan had not known just how much Keir had told his old friend. It was obvious now that Jake knew nothing of what lay behind the basic facts. So far as he was concerned Keir had asked her and she had accepted because they were meant for each other.

Keir added to the illusion by sliding a deliberate arm about her shoulders, drawing her closer to his side. The mockery in his smile was only for her. 'We both thank you,' he said. He kept the arm where it was as he added, 'Some of Regan's friends are giving us a celebration party tonight. Why don't you come along?'

'Yes, do,' said Regan, forcing herself to submit to the proprietorial gesture. She tried to infuse a genuine warmth into her tone. 'You'd be very welcome.'

From the sudden wry expression in Jake's eyes, he was not deceived. 'I'm afraid I've already got a date for tonight,' he said, 'but I appreciate the thought.' His head swivelled towards the bar. 'Is that our order they're calling?'

'I'll see to it.' Keir was on his feet even as he spoke, the tweed jacket swinging loose over a rollneck white sweater which emphasised the darkness of his hair. 'Just sit tight.'

Silence lay between the two left at the table, isolated from the hubbub going on all about them. Jake was the first to break it.

'Will you be going back to Aussie land with him, or do you plan on staying on here both of you?'

'Oh, here,' Regan said without hesitation. 'I'd never leave Cottam!'

His gaze was curious. 'Seems a shame when he's

built himself a whole new life out there. Don't suppose his father's going to want to come back now either, seeing he's married again himself. Still, I suppose you can always go out for a visit.'

'I suppose we can.' For the first time Regan actually felt relief to see Keir approaching. 'Here comes our lunch.'

The home-made pies were excellent. Regan found herself doing full justice to her own, although the accompanying french fries she left untouched. Both men ate everything before them, washing it down with lager. They had a lot to talk about, at times leaving Regan sitting on the sidelines feeling distinctly de trop.

Jake worked at the Town Hall, she learned. He was in the rates office, which fact he imparted with a wry glance in her direction.

'If you want to use me as the council's whipping boy, feel free. I'm used to it. This years rates' rise hit everybody where it hurts.'

'I wouldn't dream of it,' said Regan, who could not have told anyone what rateable value was levied on Cottam. 'You're only doing your job. Anyway, there are a lot of major projects planned which will benefit everybody, and the money has to come from somewhere.'

Jake laughed. 'I wish you'd have a word with my mother. She thinks we're spending it on banquets and new cars for the Mayor! Of course, living on the estate, we don't get hit as hard as you people.'

'Not on paper figures, maybe,' put in Keir mildly, 'but it has to be relative. I doubt if it will hit Cottam as hard as it hits your mother.'

'Well, maybe not.' Jake glanced at his watch. 'Looks like I'm going to have to love you and leave you. I was due back five minutes ago.' He hesitated only a moment before adding, 'We'll have to get together for an evening some time soon. I'm between regular girl-

friends, but I can always rustle up a partner.' His grin
was engaging. 'More unmarried girls than men in this
town, did you know that?' He was on his feet before
either could respond, lifting a hand in casual farewell.
'See you!'

Regan finished off her drink without looking at Keir,
but she could feel him watching her.

'Well?' he asked at length. 'How did you enjoy your
first taste of how the other half lives?'

'I've been in here before,' she said, and drew an
ironical smile.

'With me, a long time ago. It isn't a place your crowd
frequents.'

Regan couldn't argue with that. It wasn't what he
had been talking about anyway. 'I like your friend,'
she said. 'I didn't remember him till I saw him.'

'It wasn't obvious you'd remembered him at all,'
Keir responded dryly. 'Luckily he's not sensitive that
way. Do you want another?'

She shook her head, forcing herself to meet the grey
eyes. 'What do you plan on doing with the rest of the
afternoon?'

He let the pause lengthen with intent, smile slowly
widening as her mouth and jaw tensed. 'I'll give you a
choice,' he said in the end. 'We can either go home
and go to bed for the afternoon, or we can take a drive
and perhaps have tea out somewhere. It's up to you.'

Whether anyone sitting nearby had overheard the
offer or not, Regan didn't know and wasn't in any
mood to find out. 'All things considered, I'll take the
drive,' she returned stiffly.

'Wise girl,' he mocked. 'All right, let's move.'

To Regan's surprise, she enjoyed that afternoon.
They drove for miles through the bleak winter land-
scape, cutting down through the fringe of the Forest
of Arden into Stratford itself, to find the town quiet
and peaceful in its out-of-season garb.

'Best time of year to be here,' stated Keir over a tea of hot buttered crumpets and cakes at the Falcon. 'Must be hell living in a place like this in the summer months. It used to be just about impossible to even find a place to sit along the river bank. I don't imagine it's altered much.'

'Worse, by all accounts,' Regan responded. 'I avoid the tourist season myself. Last time I was here was the Mop Fair in October.' She pulled a face. 'It rained all day.'

'According to reports, it rained all summer. Maybe it's imagination, but I'm pretty sure it wasn't like that when I was a kid. I can remember whole weeks of sunshine!'

Regan laughed. 'Probably days seemed like weeks at that age. I know they did to me. I couldn't wait to grow up.' Catching his eye, she felt herself colour a little. 'Perhaps I tried to do it too fast.'

'Could be,' Keir agreed without particular inflection. 'What time are we going to be expected at this affair tonight?'

She accepted the change of subject without demur, aware that this was neither the time nor place to discuss their differences. 'If we're not there by nine Fiona is going to think we aren't coming at all. I've ordered an early dinner.'

'In which case we'd better not be too long before we think about moving.' He was looking at the cup in front of him, watching the liquid swirl against the sides as he stirred it. 'How many are we likely to have to face?'

'Depends on who was available when she phoned round. A dozen, at least.' Her own spirits dipped at the thought. It was in an effort to hide the fact that she said with malice, 'It isn't going to be any picnic.'

He had lifted his head and was looking back at her steadily. 'Anyone else know just why you married me?'

'No,' she admitted, and brought up her chin. 'It

doesn't have anything to do with anyone else.'

'That's all right,' he said. 'I shan't tell if you don't.' He was smiling, but faintly. 'They'll just have to take us on face value, won't they?'

Regan was quiet all the way home, aware as she had never been aware before of the man at her side. Had things been different six years ago, she thought—had *she* been different—they might have been driving around this afternoon with a couple of children in the back of the car: an ordinary, contented little family.

She smiled wryly to herself there, acknowledging the unlikelihood. Even if she had been willing to marry Keir then her father would have seen to it that she didn't. The memory of his anger when he had heard about the affair through a well-meaning friend of his was still too sharp to be put aside. Perhaps it was unfortunate that he hadn't made the discovery earlier while it was still going on. At least Keir would have been spared the ultimate humiliation. And she herself consequently spared this.

CHAPTER FIVE

REGAN had been at boarding school with Fiona Huntley, and close friends with her ever since. They had done most things together, including a twelve-month stint of flat-sharing in London while they tried out various jobs in which neither had found the kind of stimulation they were looking for. The suggestion that they return home to Cottam and start up a business of their own had been Fiona's in the first place, but one eagerly acted upon by both, resulting in the rather exclusive little boutique in nearby Warwick which they ran now on a six month on, six month off basis which elicited just the right degree of competitive spirit to keep things interesting.

It was about this that Regan was thinking on the way to Fiona's flat that evening. In less than two weeks she was due to take over for her own spell at the wheel, and right now she could hardly see her way clear. Had this marriage of hers been a normal affair she might well have contemplated selling out her share to Fiona in order to concentrate on producing the family she had promised Cottam some day. Under the circumstances, that too was going to have to wait.

Stealing a glance at the firm profile behind the wheel, she tried to envisage a future beyond this present time, failing to get past the one indisputable fact. Keir was her husband now, legally if not in any other sense. Changing that without his co-operation was not going to be easy.

So don't change it, came the thought unbidden. Settle for what you've got. You could do worse.

How much worse? she asked herself dryly, forcing

down the purely emotional response to a place where she could control it. Keir despised her as much for what she was as for what she had been, want her though he still may. Without mutual respect no relationship stood a chance of maturing into anything worthwhile, which meant they were finished before they even started. The question was, how did she go about getting rid of him?

There were already several cars parked outside the gracious, converted old house when they arrived at eight-fifty, Robin Sayers' among them. Fiona herself opened the door of her ground-floor flat, radiant in a silky blue cat-suit that matched her eyes.

'You made it!' she exclaimed with the air of one who had known full well that they would. Her interest was centered on Keir, unmasked approval in the appraisal. 'Hallo there! Remember me?'

'From afar,' he returned, completely at ease. 'I don't think we ever got round to being properly introduced.'

Fiona laughed. 'Blame this wife of yours for that. She wanted you all to herself.' She placed herself between them, taking an arm of each. 'They're all waiting to toast the happy couple. Not as many as I hoped, but enough to make it sound good. Ready?'

Regan wasn't, but there was little point in saying so. Like it or not, it had to be endured. The large, rear-facing sitting room seemed full to overflowing, in spite of Fiona's claim. There was a sudden lull in conversation as the trio appeared in the lobby doorway, every eye pivoting. Across the room, Regan saw Robin looking straight at her, the stiffness in his expression telling its own story. She tried to smile at him and found she couldn't, because no mute apology was enough for what she had done to him. She had to see him, talk to him, try to explain—though heaven only knew what she was going to say.

'Here they are!' announced Fiona somewhat unnecessarily. 'The bride and groom!'

Animation returned to the assembly as if at the pressing of a button, lifting glasses and bringing laughing comments. In the following moments Regan found herself separated from Keir, who seemed quite happy to have Fiona introduce him around. She met her own inquisitors with a bland little smile and a determination not to be thrown by anything said to her, parrying all questions regarding her sudden and secret decision with the same stock answer that it was the way they had both wanted it.

'Terribly romantic!' sighed one young woman whose own husband, Gordon, was not renowed for that particular quality. 'Coming back like that after all these years, to sweep you off your feet! Somebody was saying he used to work for Fiona's uncle.'

'He worked for the firm,' Regan admitted. 'I doubt if Fiona's uncle even knew his name.'

'And he went to Australia because you turned him down.' She didn't bother waiting for an answer. 'You must have been mad. He's so attractive! It's a wonder the Australian girls have let him get away so long!'

'Perhaps they just didn't have what he knew he could find back here,' put in Robin, coming into Regan's view from behind her somewhere. 'You should have married him the first time round, Regan. It would have saved him a long journey.'

Barbara coughed, aware as everyone here was aware of Robin Sayers' aspirations in Regan's direction. 'I must go and find Gordon before he drinks himself under the table on Fiona's champagne. It's supposed to be his turn to drive home tonight.'

Regan made herself meet the familiar hazel eyes, seeing the hurt there and knowing she was responsible. Given a definite answer from the first, there was a good chance that Robin might by now have been enamoured of some other girl. At least he would have had no cause to be looking at her now with such bitter accusation.

'I'm sorry, Robin,' she said softly. 'I haven't been very fair to you, have I?'

'No, you haven't.' His normally charming smile was missing, lending his features a melancholy air. Robin had a face like the young Byron, someone had once said. Looking now at the sensitive mouth, Regan could see what they had meant. Only Robin wasn't going to get this out of his system by sitting down and writing reams of verse about it.

'I'm sorry,' she said again, hardly knowing what else she could say. 'It—just happened, that's all.'

He studied her a moment before voicing the question. 'Is he the one you've been waiting for all these years?'

She felt a laugh bubbling up in her throat and had to fight to kill it. 'I suppose I must have been,' she said. 'Subconsciously.'

'He's not good enough for you!' He said it fiercely, surprising her a little. 'He doesn't belong at Cottam.'

Regan had thought the same thing herself, so there was no excuse for the swift sense of resentment that latter statement elicited. 'He's my husband,' she returned on a cooler note. 'That gives him the right to belong. You'll just have to accept it, Robin.'

Fiona arrived with a rush at her side, cutting off his reply. 'We're going to drink a toast,' she announced brightly. 'That means the two of you should be together while we do it. Sorry, Robin darling, but I'm going to have to take her away.'

Half leading, half pulling Regan across the room to where Keir stood with a group of people, she muttered out of the corner of her mouth. 'Better watch it with the old flames, sweetie. I've a feeling you might have a very possessive man over here.'

'Cut it out, Fi,' responded Regan in tones of impatience, and drew a speculative glance.

'Strike a nerve, did I? Well, you will do these im-

pulsive things! Not regretting it already, I hope.'
Expression bland, Fiona touched Keir's arm. 'Your
wife, sire. Cleave her to your side while I call for order,
will you?'

There was a challenge in the grey eyes as he obeyed
the injunction, drawing Regan closer to him. 'Smile,'
he murmured in her ear. 'It's supposed to be a happy
occasion.'

Looking around the gathered assemblage, Regan
briefly imagined the reaction if she told the whole truth
of her hasty marriage, and knew she didn't have the
courage. Keir was right. She had to put on a good
face in order to salvage her pride. But that didn't mean
she had to give in.

It was midnight before the party started breaking
up. Regan and Keir were among the last to leave, the
latter helping Barbara Davis steer her happily in-
ebriated husband out to the waiting car. Comparing
the two men as Keir manhandled the other bodily into
the passenger seat, Regan could only feel grateful that
Gordon was not her husband. In that state he was not
only totally unattractive, he was downright ridiculous.
And not for the first time either. She couldn't imagine
why Barbara continued to put up with it.

Barbara herself seemed to echo something of the
same sentiment as she ruefully thanked Keir for his
help.

'Regan doesn't know how lucky she is to have a man
who knows when to call enough,' she said. 'He's going
to spend the next twenty-four hours holding his head
in his hands and swearing never to touch the stuff
again, and the following twenty-four forgetting it ever
happened. Convenient at times to have a poor
memory.' Her glance swung to Regan standing waiting,
then back to the strong-featured face of the man still
holding the car door. 'I hope you'll both be very
happy.'

'Thanks.' He was smiling as he said it, but the smile didn't reach his eyes. He closed the door then as if to cut off further conversation, standing back to lift a hand in brief farewell. 'Mind how you go!'

'Poor Barbara,' commented Regan lightly as they turned away towards the Audi. 'She really does have a problem!'

'Yes.' Keir's own tone was dry. 'I wonder why he needs that kind of crutch.'

Regan shrugged. 'Does there have to be a reason? I thought people drank because they liked the stuff.'

'You would,' he came back without particular censure. 'You never had a problem in the world that couldn't be solved one way or another.'

But not always to her total satisfaction, she thought wryly, sliding into her seat. Easy enough to tell herself she wasn't going to give in to Keir back there with other people around them. Alone with him again now, she was already too well aware of the effect he had on her senses—an impact not only confined to herself, judging by the reactions of one or two others tonight. Fiona had, to put it in her own inimitable way, been knocked sideways. 'I don't blame you for snapping him up,' she had confided at one point in the evening when they were momentarily isolated from the gathering. 'He's more macho male than I've met in years!' Her blue eyes had sparkled wickedly. 'Any time you decide to throw him over just let me be the first to know.' If she knew the truth she would laugh her head off.

They were halfway back to Cottam before Regan could bring herself to speak, and when she did it was on a subdued note.

'Keir, we have to talk things out. This whole situation is quite ludicrous!'

There was nothing to be gleaned from the lean profile. 'So go ahead,' he invited.

She took a couple of long slow breaths before she started, aware that she had to make a genuine effort. 'All right, I tried to buy you, I admit that. I don't really blame you for feeling the way you do about it. I daresay I'd have felt exactly the same if it had been the other way round—except that I'd have done my retaliating another way.'

'You wouldn't have gone through with the wedding, you mean.' He sounded quite calm about it. 'I agree there were simpler ways of teaching you a lesson, but I wanted more than just a brief satisfaction. Maybe you were right this morning. Maybe Cottam and all it stands for did play a part in it. I spent twenty-four years in this town watching the way the other half lived from a distance. Could be the opportunity to get in on the act was just too much to resist.'

'And now that you are?' Regan queried softly. 'In on the act, I mean.'

It was a moment or two before he answered, the faint line drawn between his brows the only indication of his thoughts. 'It's not so different,' he said at last. 'People are people.'

'You fitted in very well tonight,' she conceded, and smiled a little. 'To the manner born, in fact.'

'Thanks.' The irony was heavy. 'That must have been a relief.'

Regan flushed. 'I didn't mean to sound patronising.'

'Didn't you?' The question held scepticism. 'You could learn a lot from your friend Fiona. She doesn't have any false values.'

The pause stretched. When she did speak again it was on a different note. 'Do you find her attractive?'

'Very,' he said. 'Most men would.'

'More so than me?'

Keir glanced at her quizzically. 'In looks you're about on a par.'

'That wasn't what I asked.'

'I know.' His mouth had a faint curve to its line. 'You're two different types. Fiona knows exactly what she wants.'

And usually gets it, Regan reminded herself, and felt her emotions tauten. Not this time, though. Keir was not on the market. Her husband: it still didn't seem real. Yet it was fact. Thinking about where they were heading right now brought a shiver of anticipation. If Keir still needed that degree of satisfaction why not give it to him—get it over with? It would be no more than the truth to say she wanted him. After last night she could hardly deny it. And afterwards? Well, that remained to be seen. They might even make something of this marriage yet.

Sullivan had left the hall and staircase lights burning, and the central heating turned up in the bedroom. Keir made no immediate attempt to touch her, shrugging off his jacket and loosening his tie as he went over to slide a wardrobe door.

Trying to adopt the same casual attitude, Regan dropped her coat carelessly over a chair and went into the bathroom, feeling her stomach muscles relax their tension a little as she closed the door softly behind her. She was acting like a bride, she thought with wry humour; any new bride faced with male intrusion on her bedtime routine for the very first time. Last night had been different in that no routine had been called for initially. While hardly wanting the same kind of treatment tonight, she had to admit that lack of time in which to consider one's actions could have its advantages. She needed the masterful touch—the removal of choice. It was the only way she could let herself go and respond to emotions of which she was basically ashamed.

Gazing at her image in the facing wall mirrors, she knew in her heart that it was no use trying to deceive herself any further. What she contemplated was no more than a calculated indulgence of needs Keir had aroused in her with such deliberation. If she had any strength of character at all she would refuse to submit to those needs.

She stayed under the shower a long time, turning on the needle sprays to full stinging strength in an effort to rid both mind and body of any lingering doubts. With her back to the cabinet door and the rush of water in her ears, she had no intimation of Keir's presence until he reached in a hand and turned off the control.

'You can't get rid of me that way,' he said. 'And I'm tired of waiting.'

The towel he placed about her was thick and soft and warm, the hands lifting her out possessed of a strength which brooked no resistance.

'Don't,' she whispered as he began to dry her. 'Keir—please!'

'You don't really mean that,' he said close by her ear. 'Do you think I can't feel what your body is telling me? You want what I want, Regan. Don't you?'

'Yes.' It was dragged from her, a small, gasping moan of a word she couldn't stop. There was no moving away from him because he held her too securely, no escaping the intimacy of those hands through the softness of the towel, the emotions flooding her. That strength of character she had so desperately sought was slipping from her, giving way to the ever more insistent little voice which asked if it really mattered. She owed Keir this. She had owed it him for years. Wasn't it time she paid her dues so that they could start afresh?

The towel slid away from her, leaving her quivering under his touch. He was naked too, she realised for the first time, and knew then that she was finished.

'Tell me,' he urged in that same throaty murmur. 'Tell me, Regan.'

She was barely conscious of saying it, knowing only

how she felt. 'I want you, Keir. Oh God, I want you!'

She was spun into his arms before the words were complete, his mouth searing hers into silence. Time dissolved as he swung her up to carry her through to the bedroom, a vortex spinning her down into mindless depths from which she never wanted to emerge.

The sun was slanting in through the side window when Regan awoke. For a moment she just lay there looking up at the ceiling and wondering why she should feel so utterly and perfectly happy, before memory brought the cause to mind with heart-jerking thoroughness.

Turning her head, she looked at the pillow at her side, seeing the dent where the other head had rested with a swelling of emotion she found difficult to contain. Last night she had been ravished in the finest sense of the word—taken to heaven and back by a man who had once loved her with his heart as well as his body. Could the younger Keir have made love to her like that? she wondered. It seemed unlikely. The man who had held her in his arms last night knew more about women than any twenty-four-year-old would have had time to learn.

The pang striking through her was not hard to identify. Jealousy of all those others who had lain in his arms and felt the same mind-bending pleasure she had experienced. Yet they hadn't been married to him, and she was. That had to make a difference. If it had been so good for her last night it must have been good for him too. That meant they had something on which to build, something vital to any marriage between two people such as themselves. Learning to love a man like Keir would not be so very difficult, not now when he had gained her respect. He should have made her respect him a long time ago before he went away. Not this way perhaps, but telling her exactly what he thought of her might have done her the world of good at the time.

She could remember him now, so still and quiet, his jaw clenching as her laugh rang out. Looking back from this distance, she could scarcely credit that he hadn't reached out and slapped her cruel young face. Only an iron control or a hurt too deep for retaliation of that sort could have turned him about and walked him away from her into the night. The next time she had seen him was in the café a few days ago.

Only a few days. It didn't seem possible that so much could have happened in so short a time. Perhaps now that the main bone of contention between them was settled they could go away somewhere—a kind of belated honeymoon. A period entirely alone together might go a long way towards sorting things out. The cottage at Ambleside, for instance. That was far enough off the beaten track. She could even cope with cooking a few meals providing he didn't expect too much.

She stirred restlessly, wishing he would hurry up and come back. He would have gone jogging, of course. They were dedicated people, these keep-fit enthusiasts. She imagined him coming through the door the way he had yesterday morning, lean and bronzed, dark hair ruffled by the breeze of his passage.

I want you, she thought, closing her eyes to trap the image. *Want* you, *want* you, *want* you!

The light knock on the door brought her starting upright in swift regret that she hadn't seized the opportunity to make herself more presentable before Keir's return. But he would hardly be knocking, she realised immediately with a smile. Not unless he'd altered radically from the man she had married. She slid down again in the bed, pulling the cover up about her bare shoulders.

'Come in,' she called.

Sullivan was carrying the usual tray, set as yesterday for two people. Obviously Keir had not seen fit as yet to have that promised word regarding breakfast downstairs. It was really her province, not his. Perhaps she should mention it now.

'Just put it on the table, will you Sullivan,' she said. 'Mr Anderson went out for a run, but he should be back any minute.'

'I don't think he went running, Miss Regan,' came the oddly hesitant response. 'His car is gone.' He picked up an envelope from the tray, carefully avoiding looking either at it or at her as he placed it within reach of her hand on the cover. 'I think this may be from Mr Anderson. It was left on the hall table.'

Regan put out fingers gone suddenly cold to take up the envelope, oblivious of the bareness of her shoulders revealed by the movement. Her name stood out boldly against the cream vellum, written in the same forceful hand which only two days ago had signed their marriage certificate. The premonition was like a scream deep inside her, hurting more than anything had ever hurt before. It took everything she had to keep her tone level.

'Thank you, Sullivan.'

Alone again, she forced herself to sit up, keeping the sheet tight across her breasts for some unearthly reason as she slit the sealed flap. The single folded sheet of notepaper inside held several paragraphs of closely written script. Regan disciplined her mind to read it, fingers creasing the edge of the sheet where she gripped it.

Since I've got what I was after, there doesn't seem very much left to say, Keir had written. *If it's any consolation, revenge isn't as sweet as it's cracked up to be in the end. I told you the truth when I said I didn't come back to Cottam with the express intention of seeking you out, although perhaps the idea was there at the back of my mind should opportunity present itself. Well, the opportunity did, and I took advantage of it, as much, I think, because of the present as the past. You're as uncaring of the feelings of others as you ever were, Regan, but at least after this you might think twice before putting yourself in the way of retaliation.*

You won't be seeing me again. I'm going back home. Annulment being clearly out of the question, it appears we either wait the statutory two years for a clean divorce, or if necessary utilise some other means. Should you not want to wait for any reason, I'll supply you with grounds to file. You'll find my full postal address on the back of the sheet.

Look after yourself, and don't forget what you've learned—if anything.

Keir.

How long she sat there staring blindly at the letter, Regan couldn't have said. It could have been hours, it could have been days. When she did stir herself it was slowly, dropping the sheet of paper to the bedcover and sliding her feet to the floor to walk over to the wardrobe wall.

The emptiness was an echo of that inside her. Gone away, never to return. How could he do this to her? How could anyone just walk away from what they had experienced together last night? It hadn't only been physical: there had been moments of tenderness, of closeness which went beyond mere sexual gratification. She remembered the sound of her name on his lips at the moment of fulfilment, as if torn from the depths of his being, the collapsing weight of his body. He had been hers then, mind and body—as totally committed as she herself had felt towards him. Or had she imagined it? Had her own emotions betrayed her? She couldn't be sure, not any more. She couldn't be sure of anything except that Keir had gone.

Fiona telephoned the following Monday afternoon.

'I thought I'd give you the weekend to yourselves,' she said cheerfully. 'Have you thought about the shop at all, or is that a silly question?'

'I've thought about it,' Regan answered. 'I'll be taking over next week as scheduled.'

'Really?' The other voice sounded faintly nonplussed. 'You know, I was pretty certain that man of yours would want you to give it up. After all, if he doesn't plan on staying in England, you're going to have to eventually, aren't you?'

'When did he tell you that?' Regan asked carefully, surprising herself by the steadiness of her voice.

'Well, he didn't exactly, I suppose. Just an impression I gained from what little he did say. Not the confiding type, is he—but I don't hold that against him. Must be great having a man as much in command of himself as Keir.' The smile could almost be seen. 'I'll bet he's fantastic in bed!'

'Fi,' Regan said numbly, 'I need to talk to you.'

'You're talking to me now.'

'Not this way. I—I have something to tell you.'

The pause was brief but telling. When Fiona spoke again it was in a different tone. 'I'll be right over.'

She arrived within half an hour, brought by Sullivan to the library where Regan sat curled in a chair by the fire.

'So what happened?' she demanded without preamble the moment they were alone. The blue eyes were concerned. 'You look washed out.'

'I feel it,' Regan confessed. 'And I'm ashamed of it. I should have more resilience.' She looked across at her friend, knowing how warm a regard that brightly careless pose concealed. It hurt to say it even now. 'Keir's left me.'

'He what?' The blankness was not assumed. Fiona shook her head. 'Look, let me get this straight. You mean he went away on business?'

'I mean he went back home to Sydney.' The laugh was brittle. 'Sounds like a modern triangle situation, doesn't it? Sydney, Australia.'

'I know where the damned place is.' Fiona paused, obviously searching for words. 'Why?' she asked bluntly at length. 'Why would he do that so soon? Did you refuse to go with him?'

'I wasn't asked.' Regan got to her feet with a jerky movement and went to pour drinks for them both, bringing back the glasses to the fireplace to press one into Fiona's hand and raise the other; lips tilting ironically. 'To the shortest marriage on record—that I know of, at any rate.'

Fiona reached out and took the glass from her, putting both down on the nearest surface. 'I'd say that was the last thing you needed right now,' she said. 'Supposing you tell me the whole story, from the beginning. Did Keir come back here to find you or didn't he?'

'Yes and no.' Regan spread her hands in apology at the look on her friend's face. 'I'm sorry, but that's the way it is. If we hadn't met by accident in the Old House last Monday I honestly don't know whether he'd have looked me up or not. From what he said, probably not.'

'You met again on Monday and married him on Thursday?' Fiona's expression was curious. 'Even faster than I imagined. When did he actually ask you?'

'He didn't. I asked him.' Regan sat down again, needing the support. 'You remember me telling you about that clause in Daddy's will?'

'You mean about selling the place up if you weren't settled down with a husband before you were twenty-five?' Fiona nodded, a certain understanding beginning to dawn. 'I remember it. I just didn't tie it in. You're saying you asked Keir to marry you just to keep the Manor?'

'At the time, yes.'

'And he knew it?'

'Yes.' Regan swallowed thickly. 'Don't look at me like that! I was pretty desperate. Keir just happened to turn up at a time when I needed somebody to help me out, that's all. It was meant to be a simple business proposition—his name in exchange for a certain sum of money.'

'Except that he turned out to have other ideas?'

Green eyes dropped to the hands clasped tightly in her lap. 'He tricked me, Fi. He tore up the draft, said he didn't want my money.'

'But he did want something.' Fiona's voice was soft. 'You don't have to tell me what, I can guess. You can hardly blame him, darling, not considering the circumstances. You gave him a bad time six years ago, and he took the opportunity to get a little of his own back.'

Regan's head had lifted. 'You sound as if you think he was in the right!'

'No, I don't, but I can sympathise to a certain extent with his feelings. You can be totally one-track when it comes to something you want. Not that I'm eligible to knock others at that particular game.' Head on one side, Fiona studied the face before her. 'Anyway, if that's all he meant to you I'd have thought you'd be glad he's gone.' The pause held deliberation. '*Was* that all he meant to you?'

'Initially, Regan said, and saw comprehension in the other eyes.

'So I was right, he *was* fantastic in bed!'

The anger was sudden and bitter, flooding from her on a tide of resentment. 'Shut up, will you! I'm sick of hearing that kind of thing from you! Don't you have any other interest in life?'

'Not a lot,' came the drawled retort, belying the

spark in Fiona's eyes. 'Dr Kinsey would have a field day with me!' The spark died as swiftly as it had flared, her mouth pulling into a wry little smile. 'Who's kidding who? It's mostly talk. I know it, and you know it. If I sound flip it's because I don't know any other way to be.'

'I'm sorry.' Regan meant it. She made a contrite little gesture. 'I don't know what made me lash out like that.'

'I do.' The reply came soft. 'You're in love with him, aren't you? That's why you're sitting here eating your heart out.'

The coppery head jerked. 'In two days? Don't be ridiculous!'

'There's nothing ridiculous about it. I could fall for a man like that in a couple of minutes, given half an excuse. And it wasn't just two days, was it? You had several weeks with him the first time. That had to provide something of a start.'

'I wasn't in love with him six years ago,' Regan protested.

'Only because you wouldn't let yourself be. He just wasn't good enough for you.' There was no malice in the statement. 'I remember the way you used to talk about him—the way you never talked about anyone else. You might have persuaded yourself you were only playing around, but he made a lot of impression on you. The mistake he made was in letting you see how he felt about you. It gave you too much of a weapon. We were both of us pretty arrogant at that age—too used to having it all our own way. I suppose the parents must shoulder a lot of the blame. I know mine would have given me anything just to keep me happy. I always swore I wouldn't make the same mistake with my own children—if I ever have any. Too much can be as bad as too little when it comes to character building.'

Regan was looking at her friend as if she had never

seen her before. 'I didn't realise you'd ever seriously contemplated settling down and having a family,' she confessed. 'You've always said marriage was out until you were at least thirty.'

'Only because I've never met any man I couldn't live without. I want that grand-slam-once-in-a-lifetime affair. The kind that has a golden wedding at the end of it.' Fiona's tone changed, briskening deliberately. 'Enough of that. It isn't me we're discussing. What do you plan on doing now?'

Regan lifted her shoulders. 'There isn't a great deal I can do except set the wheels in motion for a divorce on grounds of desertion. I suppose Matt Swain would handle that for me.'

'Do you want to divorce him?'

Regan was silent for a long moment, face still. 'Not like this,' she admitted at last.

'Then go and tell him so.'

'To Australia!'

'Why not? What's a few thousand miles to a woman in love?' The tone was light, but the blue eyes were serious. 'If he's worth having he's worth fighting for. It might even be what he's hoping for—proof that you care. What you have to ask yourself is, do you care enough?'

Did she? Regan thought back over the past week, visualising the man who had changed her life, remembering the things he had said to her, done to her; the feel of his hands, the sound of his voice, the emotions he had aroused. But there was more to it than that, wasn't there? To follow him now would be like begging for crumbs. He had made his true feelings about her plain, and she had to accept it. At least she still had Cottam. No one could take that away from her now.

'It wouldn't work,' she said. 'You have to see that. If he cared about me at all he wouldn't have left in such a fashion.' She stilled Fiona's intended reply with a small movement of her hand. 'No, that's it. I don't want to discuss it any more.' Her smile was deliberately bright. 'About the shop—would you like me to take over this weekend? Give you a little more time to pack.'

'I can fly to California any day of the week,' Fiona came back on an odd note. 'You sure you won't change your mind?'

Regan shook her head. 'Not a chance. I've got the house, and that's all I really care about.'

She kept right on telling herself that over the next couple of days, making herself believe it. Matt Swain's visit on the Wednesday came as something of a surprise as he had not intimated that he needed to see her again. He looked ill at ease, she thought, viewing him over coffee in the library. Like a man about to do something he didn't like, yet found unfortunately necessary.

'What is it, Matt?' she asked at length when the small talk was exhausted. 'What went wrong?'

His smile was wry. 'So much for my professional impassivity! I thought I was building up to it gradually.' He hesitated before going on, eyes not quite meeting hers. 'I heard this new husband of yours went back to Australia. Is it true he won't be coming back to Cottam again?'

Who? Regan wondered briefly. The Sullivans? Fiona? She shrugged inwardly. Did it really matter? 'No,' she said, 'he won't.'

'Oh dear!' He sounded both unhappy and worried. 'That makes things rather difficult.'

'You mean about Cottam?' Alarm shot through her, bringing her to the edge of her seat. 'Matt, I fulfilled my obligations in marrying. The will said nothing about him having to stay on!'

'I know,' he returned. 'That isn't quite the point.' Again the hesitation, so uncharacteristic of his usual brisk style of delivery. 'You see, it's a matter of his signature on some essential papers. I'm afraid we have to have it before things can proceed any further.'

'His signature?' Regan stared at him in a mixture of puzzlement and growing dismay. 'You can't be serious!'

'Indeed I am.' This time he sounded more like himself, bringing out each word with precise intent. 'Without it you're back where you started. I'm sorry, Regan, but it never occurred to me to warn you against letting the man you married go away too soon.'

The rebuke warmed her cheeks, the more so because she knew it was well deserved. 'I cheated, didn't I?' she said ruefully. 'I suppose this is a judgment on me.'

His nod seemed to signify agreement, but there was fondness in his eyes. 'I've known you since you were born,' he said unexpectedly. 'You know I'd do anything I can towards your happiness. You must go to him, Regan, persuade him to come back.'

'Why?' she demanded. 'Why do I have to go to him? If his signature is all that's required the papers could be sent out to him.'

'I'm afraid not. They have to be witnessed in person.' He spread his hands. 'I wish there were some other way, but there isn't. James tried to cover every eventuality, including making sure that the man you married wasn't in it just for the money. You've just about a month to do it in, so you can't afford to take too much time deciding.'

'I can't.' It came out as a whisper. 'I can't go after him!'

'Then you lose the house,' Matt came back flatly. 'Are you willing to settle for that?'

'No!' Regan made a sudden helpless little gesture, sinking back into her seat. 'Oh, Matt, I've made such a mess of things! What am I going to do?'

Visibly he hardened himself. 'I've told you what you have to do. Bring Keir Anderson back here. There's no other way.'

Regan closed her eyes, seeing the lean, hard features as clearly as if he were standing in front of her now. Bring him back how?

'All right,' she said huskily, I'll go.'

CHAPTER SIX

THE humid heat struck her the moment she stepped out of the plane, making her thankful for her foresight in packing the lightweight linen dress in her hand baggage. After twenty minutes in the well-equipped first class toilet before breakfast, she had felt refreshed and revitalised from the rigours of the long journey; ready to face whatever she had to face. Right now she wasn't quite so confident. She was a long, long way from home.

It had taken her almost a week to prepare herself for the trip because of the necessary paperwork entailed. That left her with just three weeks in which to accomplish her aim. Coming over, she had decided that a straight approach was the only one possible. She had to throw herself on Keir's charity and hope that his vengeance had been appeased enough to indulge her need. It wasn't going to be easy laying her pride at his feet in such a way, but if it meant the difference between having Cottam and not having it, then she would force herself to go through with it. She would pay for the return trip, of course, and this time he might be persuaded to accept a sum in compensation for his time and trouble. The only price she would not be prepared to pay was the one already taken. She would, Regan told herself numbly, rather lose the house than suffer that kind of humiliation again.

Queueing to go through the formalities of landing, she noted the vitality which seemed to exude from the obvious natives of this sun-kissed land, a confidence in male and female alike which made them stand out from other nationalities present. Everywhere there was the healthy glow of tanned skins, showing up the winter palor of visitors like herself to disadvantage, making her want to find a beach and lie on it until she too turned that beautiful shade of golden brown. Difficult to realise that it was still midwinter back home. The temperature had been in the thirties when she had left London. Here it had to be around ninety, probably a great deal more in the full blast of the morning sun. The humidity out here was more than a little oppressive, but no doubt one became accustomed to that too in time. It was simply a matter of knowing what you were up against and dressing accordingly—like those youngsters over there in their tiny shorts and cotton tops. Fortunately Regan had packed a minimum of man-made fibres. They might be easier to keep looking spick and span, but they retained too much heat for comfort.

With her luggage claimed and piled on to a trolley, she made her way from the terminal building to look for a taxi rank. First she had to find a hotel, then she could make a plan of campaign. The suburb where Keir had his address was on the north shore, the name 'Beach Drive' suggesting a fairly close proximity to the sea. What kind of dwelling it might be she had no fixed idea. Hardly a large one, she imagined, for a man living on his own. Not her concern anyway. She hoped she wouldn't be here long enough to see much of it.

The first rush of incoming travellers had mercifully diminished, leaving several taxis standing in rank waiting for fares. The leading driver was leaning nonchalantly against the bonnet of his vehicle reading a newspaper. A wiry man in the mid-fifties, he made little concession towards formality in dress, his shirt hanging free of his trousers for coolness.

'Okay,' he said without overmuch enthusiasm in answer to Regan's request. 'Sling your stuff in the boot. It's open.'

'Aren't you going to do it?' she demanded in some indignation as he slid into the driving seat, and received a glance of bland indifference.

'I'm a driver, not a baggage handler, lady. You want help with that, you go find yourself a porter.'

She hadn't seen any porters, she was about to retort, but stopped herself. There was no point in making an issue of it. Not according to all she had heard. Australians had a bee in their collective bonnet about equality; not of the sexes but of the classes. Lifting suitcases into a boot smacked of servility, therefore it was out. So, she reflected fumingly, was common courtesy, by the look of it!

'Here, let me do it,' said another voice on a note of laconic amusement, and the driver of the next vehicle in line stepped forward with a grin to oblige, swinging her suitcase easily. He was younger than the other man, and built like an athlete, though no less casually dressed. 'English, aren't you?' he added, shutting down the boot lid. His glance was frankly appraising. 'First time out?'

Regan nodded, wondering whether to tip him, but a certain expression in the blue eyes decided her against it. She smiled at him with warmth instead. 'Thanks. You just tipped the balance back in favour.'

'Any time you're passing.' He lifted a hand in friendly farewell. 'See you around.'

'Any price range in mind?' asked her driver as she climbed into the rear seat. He sounded quite unaffected by anything he might have overheard; certainly in no way ashamed. 'Medium? Expensive?'

'The best,' she stated. 'And preferably with a view of the harbour.' If she was going to have little time for sightseeing at least she could have that much. This was Sydney, Australia, the other side of the world. Whatever her reasons for being here, she could hardly remain indifferent to that fact.

The city itself did not disappoint her; a silhouette like a miniature New York, a maze of streets, a haphazard yet fascinating mixture of old and new. Seen from the window of her hotel room, the beauty of the harbour went beyond all expectations. One could imagine the sheer spectacle of that approach from the sea; coming in through the Heads to the white sails of the Opera House on the left bank, the soaring span of the Harbour Bridge, the sunlight glinting from a thousand windows, sparkling on water as blue as the sky. Perhaps if everything went right there might be time to take a few days to explore, to discover a little more about this outpost of civilisation. If everything went right.

It was still only a little after ten-thirty. A shower and a change of clothing would take her no more than ten or fifteen minutes. Why wait for tomorrow, she thought with a firming resolve, when she had the whole day ahead? Strike now before her nerve failed her altogether.

·She was in another taxi speeding across the bridge by eleven, following the Pacific Highway through residential suburbs of houses ranging from the small to the frankly huge, the old to the new. Some of the former, she reckoned, had probably been here for years before the city had stretched this far. That would explain the apparent incongruity of tin-roofed bungalows sitting cheek by jowl with palatial neighbours. It certainly added contrast.

When they eventually turned off, it was towards the sea down an unmetalled road signposted by a bare board set on a post hammered into the sandy ground. The house lay around a bend, set back amidst a small stand of pine so that it lay partially in shade, the sea beyond it a vast blue expanse bound only by the jut of a low headland in the middle distance. A big house, long, low and graceful, with windows stretching from ground to brown-tiled over-jutting roof. Built within the last couple of years, Regan guessed, and at no small cost by any standards. The lawns reaching down to the perimeter wall had a green perfection only a constant supply of water could bring. Even as she watched, hidden sprinklers came into play, tossing shimmering droplets across the expanse to fall just short of the curving driveway.

'There must be some mistake,' she said to the driver. 'This can't be the place I want.'

'There's only this place here,' pointed out the man with indisputable logic. 'Beach Drive you said, Beach Drive it is.'

'Then there must be another.'

He looked at her through the driving mirror, a long-suffering look. 'What name?'

'Name? Oh—Anderson.'

A jerk of a thumb indicated the direction in which her eyes should travel. The nameplate on the mail box a few feet away from where they sat was clearly visible. There was no mistake.

Feeling decidedly confused, Regan got out of the car and paid the man, turning back again to gaze at the house in long hesitation as he pulled away. Keir had not been lying when he had said he didn't need her money; no one who lived in a place like this could be short of that commodity. It altered everthing, and not for the better. If hard cash held no inducement she was left with only the appeal to his better nature, and right now that seemed a less than hopeful proposition. But she had to try. She hadn't come all this way to give up so easily.

Somehow it had not occurred to her that there might be no one at home, but when her second ring of the doorbell elicited no response she was forced to that conclusion. She should have kept the taxi standing by until she had made certain, she realised, but it was too late for that now. She would simply have to wait around for Keir to turn up.

The first thing she had to do was to get out of this sun before she fried. No doubt there would be somewhere to sit around the rear of the house, always providing she could gain entry. Hot, and getting hotter by the minute, she made her way along the front past the screened and draped windows, traversing the deep end wall to pass through a stone archway on to an open view of the sea. The height of the large wooden deck built out from the back of the house obscured the immediate grounds. It was only on mounting the steps leading up on to it that Regan saw the pool laid out below and beyond, the gaily coloured umbrellas and long loungers.

Keir was standing on the edge looking down into the water, his back to where she stood. He was wearing white trunks brief enough to conceal only the same narrow strip about his loins, the rest of the superbly fit body tanned mahogany and gleaming faintly with oil.

Looking at him, Regan felt a sudden dryness come into her throat, the ache start deep, and fought to control it. That part of their relationship was over, once and for all. She was here to gain his co-operation, nothing else.

He turned quite suddenly, as if feeling her gaze, freezing into stillness when he saw her standing there above him. It seemed an age before he moved, making for the steps. His expression when he reached her was hard to decipher, but there was little or no surprise. He might almost have been expecting her.

Regan spoke first, voice jerky. 'You don't have to concern yourself, I haven't come to make trouble. I wouldn't have come at all if I didn't need you to complete your side of the bargain.'

He said nothing for a moment, but she sensed the hardening in him. When he did speak it was on a measured note. 'You don't change, do you, Regan?'

'Not easily,' she agreed. 'Certainly not *that* easily.' She watched the narrowing of his eyes fatalistically, knowing she was going about this in entirely the wrong way yet unable to help herself. 'You had all *you* wanted, but you didn't wait around long enough to pay your own dues.'

The lift of his brow was sardonic. 'I was under the impression all you needed was my signature on a set of marriage lines. Did I forget to sign them?'

'No, but it's your signature I still need.' She steadied herself, aware that she was being a fool. She had to approach this thing slowly, a bit at a time. 'Some legal papers,' she added, this time choosing her words with care. 'I didn't know about them myself until my solicitor told me. It's essential you sign them, Keir. Otherwise I don't get to keep Cottam.'

'And that's all you really care about.' His shrug held a certain weariness. 'Why make the trip at all? You could have sent them by post.'

'And risk losing them?' She shook her head. 'I had to come myself.'

'All for a house.'

'Not just any house,' she returned shortly. 'My home. It's been in the family for three generations. I don't intend losing it now.'

'No,' he said, 'I can see that.' He sounded totally unemotional. 'You'd better let me see what I'm supposed to put my name to.'

'I didn't bring them with me.' She lacked the courage to add the rest. 'I—I wasn't sure you'd be here.' She turned her head sharply at the sound of car engines. 'Are you expecting visitors?'

'Barbecue lunch,' he said succinctly. 'They'll be coming in droves from now on. You'll have to hang on till I can find time to run you back to town.' Registering the question which sprung in her eyes, he

shook his head. 'Nobody knows I got myself a wife
while I was over in England. They don't have to know
now. I'll introduce you as a friend come to say hallo.'
The irony bit. 'Just a flying visit.'

There was no time to reply, to argue about it, because people were coming through the archway from
the front of the house, young people ranging from
Regan's own age to around Keir's. They were all of
them dressed casually in shorts or jeans, making Regan
feel distinctly overclad in her tan cotton. In a moment
the deck was awash with healthy brown bodies, the
morning peace shattered by a dozen voices all claiming
their right to be heard.

Introductions, Regan found, took place on their own
after the initial couple or so, her presence accepted with
a friendly ease which put her at hers. More people
arrived, overflowing into the pool and over the surrounding grass, stripped down to the bare minimum
of clothing now and totally unselfconscious about it.

'I'm afraid I didn't bring a suit with me,' Regan
admitted in answer to one young woman's suggestion
that she would be more comfortable herself out of that
dress.

'No problem,' answered the other, pulling a couple
of scraps of yellow material out of her roomy string
bag. 'I always carry a spare. You might have to pull
the bottom tapes a bit tighter,' she added, running an
assessing eye over Regan's figure. 'I think I'm a bit
wider in the hip. Same size boobs, though.' Her grin
was infectious. 'I always thought you Poms were all
flat-chested.'

'Only the men,' Regan came back, copying her
mood. She cast a glance around, failing to find who
she sought. 'Do you know where I can change? I
haven't been here before.'

'I'll show you,' the other girl offered.

She chose a white-painted door leading in from a

corner of the deck on to a corridor, opening another about halfway down the latter to usher Regan through into a sizeable bedroom.

'Guestroom,' she said. 'Nobody's likely to walk in on you here.' She perched herself comfortably on a corner of a built-in unit as Regan began to unbutton her shirtwaister, long shapely legs swinging. 'Did you just meet Keir while he was over this time, or did you two know one another before?'

With no way of guessing which way Keir would have told the story, Regan had to take a chance on the answer. 'We knew one another before,' she said. 'I couldn't pass through Sydney without paying him a call.'

'You're not here for long, then?'

'Only a few days.' Regan mentally crossed her fingers. 'It's just a flying visit.'

'So Keir said.' The pause held a certain innuendo. 'He's a great guy, isn't he?'

Regan forced a laugh. 'For a Pommy, you mean?'

'Oh, that's so much talk. He's one of us now. He might have to travel farther afield now that he's gone into Europe, but he'll always come back here in the end. Australia gave him his start, and he's not the kind to forget it.'

'What exactly does he do?' asked Regan before she had time to think about it. She saw the other's change of expression and shrugged with what lightness she could muster. 'We never got around to discussing his work.'

Blue eyes darkened a little, although the smile remained constant. 'I expect you had other things in mind. Ever heard of Airflow?'

'No,' Regan admitted. 'Is that the company he works for?'

'That's the company he is.' There was a faint pro- prietorial pride in the statement. 'He developed a revolutionary new air-conditioning unit that's smaller, cheaper to install and half the price to run, of any comparable system. Three years since he went into the market, and he's never looked back. I shouldn't think he ever will, not while the sun's still up there. He turned down a huge take-over offer only last week.'

Little wonder he hadn't been interested in her measly ten thousand, Regan thought wryly. His was the success story of the decade if all this girl said was true. She certainly seemed to know a lot about it. On the pretext of checking the fit of the brief bikini through the long mirror set into the wall close by, she made a swift appraisal of the blonde-haired Amazon still seated on the unit behind her. Australian girls were among the most naturally beautiful in the world, she had read somewhere, and this one certainly appeared to bear out that claim. Keir's type definitely. She wondered how close they really were.

'You know, I don't think I got your name,' she said on a casual note which entirely belied her emotions. 'There were so many people all arriving at once out there.'

'It's Jane,' the other girl said. 'Jane Denver.' The blue eyes were not deceived. 'I've known Keir for years, but we're not lovers, if that's what you want to know. My boy-friend wouldn't like it.' She slid to her feet, the smile still friendly. 'If you're ready let's get back to the eats. I'm ravenous!'

Regan followed her slowly, conscious of having betrayed more than she intended. She was possessive about Keir, there was no getting away from that. Yet she had no right to be. He was his own master; he had made that perfectly clear.

The smell of cooking steak filled the air outside. Left temporarily alone, Regan knelt on the bench seat running along one side of the deck and watched the 'cooks' at work around the brick barbecue pits. Keir was one of them, totally at home among these people—even looking like one of them in his lean brown fitness. He had the knack of fitting in wherever he happened to be, she acknowledged, recalling the party Fiona had given them, though of the two occasions he no doubt preferred this. She did herself, if it came to that. Fresh air, sunshine, good company—they were all plusses.

'You'd better watch the sun on that skin of yours,' advised the fair-haired young man in the blue trunks leaning on the rail close by. 'It can be lethal even when you're used to it.'

Regan turned her head to glance at him, liking what she saw. A couple of years or so older than herself, she guessed, and built along the same lines as all the other men here. No doubt there were Australians who were overweight and flabby, but not among this group. Perhaps, she thought whimsically, it was a condition of entry.

'I tan easily in spite of my hair,' she said, smiling at him. 'And it feels so marvellous straight from a British winter! You're Don, aren't you? I don't remember your surname.'

'Never use it,' he said. 'Don will do fine.' He dropped on to the seat beside her, manner relaxed and friendly. 'Known Keir long?'

'Long enough.' She knew her face had stiffened. This pretence was beginning to get her down, yet what other alternative was there? It was too late for the truth, and too difficult to explain anyway. She was stuck with the part Keir had given her to play.

'He's a bit of a cult figure round here,' Don went on, apparently oblivious to any tension. 'Got it together real fast.'

'Do you resent that?' asked Regan softly, and received a straight look.

'Because he's not an Aussie? No, he's doing a good job. Brought air within reach of a lot more people.

The way things are going he'll be a millionaire before he's been in business five years. He's going to have a hard job of it trying to stay a bachelor, you take my word!'

'There's more to a man than money,' she came back with control. 'Are you married?'

He hesitated before answering. 'Separated,' he admitted at length. 'Mutual agreement, so don't bother with the sympathy.'

'I wasn't going to offer any.' Regan's pause was brief. 'Were you married long?'

'Three years. We're coming up for a divorce this year.' He sounded quite matter-of-fact about it. 'Going to be a long time before I put my head in that noose again!'

That was a sentiment with which Regan felt in total accord—except that she didn't even have her freedom in sight yet.

'Come and have a dip before we eat,' invited Don, standing up again. 'It's as hot as hell up here.'

It wasn't all that much cooler in the water, although the wetness was pleasant. Regan came out laughing, squeezing the ends of her hair and leaving it to drip dry the way the others were doing. No need of towels where the sun was hot enough to do the job. The bikini was almost dry on her before they reached the barbecue area.

Keir was serving out steaks as they were cooked, leaving the recipients to take their pick of the accompaniments spread out along the trestle table behind the pit. Holding out her plate, Regan steeled herself to meet the grey eyes as they skimmed the length of her body.

'Make mine a small one, please,' she requested with what lightness of tone she could muster. 'I'm not really all that hungry.'

'You're starting to burn,' he said. 'Find something

to cover your shoulders with.'

She was beginning to feel it, but his brusqueness made her stubborn. 'I'm quite all right, thanks. I never burn.'

His shrug disclaimed responsibility. 'Be it on your own head.'

'You two have a row before we turned up?' asked Don with some interest as they moved away from the table. 'It's the first time I ever heard him sound as short.'

'Probably the heat getting to him,' she said with an innocent air. 'I'd only just arrived myself.'

The heat continued to get to her during the following hour. Feeling the growing tightness on her shoulders and back, she knew she was being an idiot, yet she still refused to give in and retire to the shade. It was almost a relief when people started to leave, surfing, it appeared, being the next order of the day. She shook her head without regret when Don asked if she would like to join them.

'I don't have time,' she lied, 'although I'm sure it must be great fun. Anyway, I have to go and change. I borrowed the suit from Jane Denver.'

'She's already left,' Don said. 'Leave it here. She'll pick it up when she's ready. Sure you won't change your mind? I've a spare board on the car. Providing you're a fair swimmer you'd soon get the hang of it.'

'Not in one afternoon,' put in Keir, joining them out of nowhere. 'Anyway, we have some things to discuss.'

'That mean you're not coming down either?' Don sounded disappointed. 'You still owe me one, sport!'

'Next week,' came the easy reply. 'I don't leave till the Monday.'

'You're on.' To Regan he added, 'Come with him if you're still around, then you'll see some real surfing. He's only on the winning end right now because I pulled a muscle last weekend.'

'I'm hoping to be back home by then,' she said, and wished she could add that the same went for Keir. What had he meant by leaving on the Monday? Leaving for *where* on the Monday?

It was another half an hour before everyone had gone, not to the beach adjoining which apparently had no surf, but farther along the coastline to some place called Curl Curl. The debris from the barbecue had been cleared away by a dozen willing pairs of hands, leaving the deck and surrounding areas as clean and as tidy as when Regan first arrived.

Her clothing was in the guestroom where she had left it, but she made no immediate attempt to change, gingerly flexing her shoulders as she tried to assess the extent of the damage through the mirror. She was going to suffer for her stupidity tonight; the heat radiating from her now told her that much.

Keir spoke from the doorway behind her. 'I've run a cool bath and put in some bicarb. It will take the heat out. Stay in it for at least twenty minutes.'

'I'll be all right,' she said without turning, and heard his teeth come together.

'Do it! It's a couple of doors down.'

She waited until his footsteps had faded away before moving to comply, knowing there was sense in what he said. The bathroom was large and luxuriously appointed, with a separate shower cabinet in addition to the semi-sunken bath. Stripping off the bikini, she lowered herself slowly and tenderly into the water, stretching out her legs to let her shoulders slide under the surface. That was better. With any luck she'd lose nothing more than a few patches of skin which would be covered up anyway when she got back home.

When was the question, she thought pessimistically. She still had to tell Keir the truth of the matter. Nothing she had said or done today had been of any help to her plans. If she wanted him to comply she was going to have to show a little more circumspection in her dealings with him. It was, after all, no small thing she was asking.

He was standing at the bedroom window when she eventually went back there, wrapped securely in one of the thick white towels. The glance he turned on her was cool.

'I brought some after-sun cream to rub in,' he said. 'You'd better let me do your back.'

'No!' The denial broke from her before she could stop it. She gathered herself to add stiffly, 'I can manage.'

'Not unless you're a contortionist.' He advanced on her, picking up a large plastic bottle from the dressing unit in passing, mouth tightening as she took an involuntary step backwards. 'Stop being an idiot, Regan. Without this you're not going to be able to move by morning.'

'I don't want you touching me,' she flung at him. 'I didn't come here for that!'

'You've already made that pretty obvious.' Eyes glittering, he seized her by an elbow and turned her about, pressing her down to a seat on the edge of the bed. 'Let the towel drop or I'll take it off you altogether. You're not going to finish up in a doctor's surgery through sheer stupidity!'

Biting her lip, Regan did as he instructed, fighting the impulse to cover her breasts with her hands. She was showing nothing that he hadn't seen before, and in far more shameful circumstances. She must have been the easiest conquest he had ever made, she thought with bitterness.

Steeled against it though she was, the touch of his hands made her catch her breath. He was very gentle, smoothing the lotion over the reddened skin from the top of her shoulders right down to her waistline, easing the tight drawn feeling with every stroke. Aware that he could see her face through the mirror opposite if he glanced up, she made every effort to keep it impassive, but there was no disguising the tremors running through her.

'That's enough,' she said at length through clenched teeth. 'I can manage the rest myself.'

Keir handed her the bottle over her shoulder without argument, expression revealing nothing. 'I'll see you out back,' he said, and went.

The lotion helped, but it still took her some effort to ease herself into her clothing. Her bra she left off altogether, folding it into a neat little parcel and putting it in her handbag.

Inevitably the moment came when she had to leave the room and go to find Keir. There was no point in having him drive her back to her hotel to look at papers which simply weren't there. She had to tell him exactly what she wanted of him, and she had to do it now.

She found him waiting for her on the deck, ready to go in light slacks and shirt. He straightened away from the rail when he saw her.

'We won't hang around out here,' he said. 'Where are you staying?'

It was hard to find the words. 'It isn't as simple as it sounds,' she got out. 'The papers you need to sign aren't at the hotel.'

He looked at her for a lengthy moment without moving, a light of understanding beginning to dawn in his eyes. 'Just tell it the way it is,' he suggested dryly. 'It will save a lot of time.'

'All right, I don't have them with me at all. They have to be witnessed.'

'By whom?'

'Matt Swain, my solicitor. He wouldn't let them out of his hands.'

'Just let me get this straight,' said Keir. 'You came

all this way to persuade me to go back with you just to sign something I should have signed while I was over there. A bit shortsighted of you, wasn't it?'

'I told you, I didn't even know about it until Matt told me last week.' Regan was trying hard to stay cool and calm about it and only just succeeding. 'He wasn't to realise you'd take off at a moment's notice the way you did.'

'Not even a moment,' he reminded her brutally. 'You didn't merit any consideration then, and you still don't.'

She stared at him, heart sinking. 'Does that mean you refuse?'

'It means I don't see any good reason to hare halfway across the world again.'

'We made a bargain!'

'Which I kept. You asked me to marry you, and I did. That certificate's the only proof you need.'

'You don't believe me, do you?' Her voice was low. 'You think I'm making it all up. Why? What could I possibly hope to gain?'

'No, I don't think you're making it up.' Keir sounded suddenly weary of the whole subject. 'I can't imagine why I'd need to sign anything, but if you say it's so it's so. You're just asking too much, that's all.'

'I'm fighting for my home,' Regan came back desperately. 'If I fail to get those papers signed before my birthday in three weeks' time, everything I've done has been for nothing.'

'That's not true,' he said. 'There's no court in the land would uphold that will of your father's.'

'Except that I'm not willing to drag it through the courts.'

He studied her for a moment or two with an expression difficult to define before making an abrupt movement. 'Let's get out of this sun.'

Furnished in pale green and white with touches of apricot, the big L-shaped living room gave an impression of coolness even without the benefit of the softly humming air-conditioning. Invited to a seat, Regan refused, aware that if she once sat down she might not want to get up again. Her body was burning beneath her clothing, her head ached with a dull persistent throb and there was a growing sense of nausea. She had to get this settled and get back to the hotel before Keir guessed how she was feeling. She couldn't be ill here.

'I realise it's asking a lot to make that journey again so soon,' she said, trying to keep any trace of abjection out of her voice, 'but we could fly Concorde from Singapore. That would cut down on the time.'

'Not enough to meet my commitments.' He shook his head. 'It's no use, Regan. I'm due in Brisbane next Monday and Cairns on the Wednesday, to say nothing of others right here in Sydney this week. There's no way I'm going to start shifting that schedule around.'

Regan believed him; when he spoke like that there was no way she could not believe him. It left only one last chance.

'What about the week after?' she asked. 'I'll be twenty-five on the twenty-second of March. That means we have until the twenty-first.' The nausea was getting worse, washing over her in waves. She gritted her teeth against it. 'I'd be out of your life then, for good. We can file for an official separation order to help things along at the right time.'

His move to put the back of a hand against her throbbing forehead took her by surprise. His hand felt cool to her skin, his touch gentle.

'You're running a temperature,' he said. 'The best place for you is bed in a cool darkened room until you start feeling better.'

Denying her condition would have been a waste of

time. She said weakly, 'I have to get back to the hotel.'

'Not like that you don't.' Hand firm on her arm, he turned her about, urging her towards the door. 'We'll talk this over later.'

The room to which he took her was the same one in which she had changed. It was Keir who turned back the light cover and drew the blind, eyeing her in the resulting dimness.

'You'd be better with your dress off again,' he observed matter-of-factly. 'Can you manage?'

She was beyond caring any more, eager only to lay her head on a cool pillow and close her eyes. 'If you'd just help me with the zip.'

He did better than that, easing the garment down over her hips so that she could step out of it, then leaving her to slide into the bed and pull the cover over herself while he hung it away in the closet.

'I'm going to bring you some Codeine,' he said when he emerged again. 'It should help the headache if nothing else.'

'How do you know I've got a headache?' Regan murmured as he moved towards the door.

He answered without pausing. 'Because that's how too much sun affects people. It happens to a lot of newcomers to the country.'

'Particularly those who won't listen to advice.' She moved an apologetic hand. 'I never meant to cause you all this trouble.'

His tone was sardonic. 'I'm sure you didn't.'

He was back inside half a minute bearing a glass of water and two white tablets, lifting her to take them with a supporting arm behind her shoulders. She saw his eyes rest briefly on the curve of her breasts pushing against the thin sheet as she lay down again, saw the faint ironic smile touch his mouth, then he was gone, leaving her alone in the darkened room with her thoughts.

CHAPTER SEVEN

SHE must have slept eventually, for when she next opened her eyes the room was filled with a deep golden glow which penetrated even the pulled blind. The headache was gone, she realised thankfully, testing by moving her head on the pillow, and so too had the nausea. Probably as much a product of jet lag as anything else, she reasoned. All she had needed was a few hours' sleep.

It was only when she attempted to sit up that she remembered her sunburn. Despite the treatment Keir had administered, her shoulders and back had stiffened, making movement of any kind painful. Dressing was going to be difficult, especially when it came to getting her arms back to fasten her zip. Considering the way she had allowed Keir to help her out of the dress, she supposed it was only common sense to ask his help again, yet the thought went against the grain. Before she saw him she had to be in command of herself, physically and emotionally. It was the only way she was going to be able to cope.

The tap on the door was designed to alert only the already awake. Unprepared for confrontation, Regan pretended not to hear it, closing her eyes again hastily when the door opened.

Keir's movement across to the bed was almost noiseless, his pause beside it seemingly endless. She could feel him looking at her, and fought hard to keep her lids from fluttering, wishing he would go away and leave her alone for a little while longer. She wanted to be on her feet and fully clothed when she spoke to him again, not lying here half naked and defenceless.

The touch of his fingertips against her skin was

gentle enough to have been imagined. Only when the sheet began to slide slowly downwards did she come alive to his intention, and her hands come up involuntarily to clutch the material to her.

'I thought that might bring you round,' he said on a dry note. 'Contrary to general opinion, sleepers breathe faster and lighter than you were doing. How's the head?'

'All right.' Her own tone was abrupt. 'I suppose if I'd really been asleep you'd have carried on!'

'I doubt it. I'm hardly so starved of a sight of female anatomy.' He paused briefly, still standing too close to the bed for comfort. 'Do you feel well enough to get up, or shall I bring you some supper right here?'

'I'm getting up.' She ran her tongue over her teeth and made a grimace of distaste. 'I don't suppose you've a spare toothbrush hanging around?'

'You could always use mine,' he said with mockery. 'I don't mind. If you're going to make tracks for the bathroom I'll find you a robe to slip on.'

The one he brought out of the closet was in white terry towelling, and a small enough size to cause speculation. Regan made no comment as he tossed it over the end of the bed, but her chest muscles contracted. So what? she asked herself in an effort to rationalise her emotions. This was a guestroom. No doubt others had slept here before her. Keir's stepmother, for instance. She could quite easily have left the robe behind—perhaps even kept it here permanently against future visits. One thing she would not do was ask who it belonged to.

'If you need any help,' said Keir from the door, 'just yell. I'll only be in the kitchen.'

She made it to the bathroom without mishap, flexing her shoulders as she went. It wasn't really too bad now she was on the move again. With any luck and some more of that after-sun lotion, she might even escape the worst of the peeling.

The sight of the small burgundy leather case sitting waiting on a stool brought her up short in the doorway. The last time she had seen it had been in her room back at the hotel. There would have been time for Keir to fetch it, of course, while she had been asleep, but why would he bother? She was hardly going to be here long enough to have any dire need of toiletries.

Acting on half-formed suspicion, she retraced her steps to the bedroom and opened up the walk-in closet, viewing the second and larger piece of luggage with indrawn breath. He had indeed been busy!

She found the kitchen by process of elimination, looking at the table laid ready for a meal in the wide, jutting window without really seeing it. Keir was standing by a work surface tossing a salad in a large wooden bowl with a deftness which bespoke long practice. He spoke without turning round.

'I thought we'd eat in here for convenience. I hope you like your salad dressed?'

The words came short and sharp. 'What are you playing at, Keir?'

Typically he made no attempt to prevaricate. 'I saw no point in leaving it till after dark. I found the name of the hotel in your handbag along with your passport. Once I proved who I was, there was no difficulty getting your things.' He looked at her then, expression totally lacking in apology. 'A little companionship isn't a high price to pay for what you're asking of me.'

'Companionship?' There was a sudden tremor in her voice. 'Is that all you want?'

His smile came slow. 'It will do until you get over that sunburn, then we'll see. You can't expect to get everything for nothing. Are you ready to eat now, or would you rather be dressed? It's all cold so nothing's going to spoil.'

'I won't stay,' Regan said low-toned. 'Not on those terms.'

'You don't have any choice,' Keir pointed out, 'Not if you want me on that plane in two weeks' time. You'll be on your own most of the time anyway. I leave for Brisbane next Monday, remember.'

Regan gazed at him helplessly, sensing his complete immovability. She had asked for it, she supposed, coming here like this, yet what alternative had there been? If she wanted to keep Cottam she had to go along with him—or at least appear to do so.

'All right,' she said on a note of resignation. 'You win. Just give me ten minutes to freshen up.'

It took longer than that, of course, owing to the painful tightness in her back and shoulders. Back in the bedroom, she opened her suitcase and found a white halter-necked sundress which would leave the most tender parts of her skin untouched, sliding the smooth cotton up over slender hips. Devoid of make-up apart from a touch of palest pink lipstick, her face in the mirror looked oddly vulnerable. She avoided looking at it again as she trod into high-heeled mules, concentrating instead on calming her nerves. There was nothing to be afraid of in what Keir was demanding from her; nothing she hadn't experienced before. Which was exactly why she was afraid, she acknowledged in a sudden burst of honesty. She wanted Keir to make love to her again—had wanted it since the first moment she had set eyes on him this morning. Yet that way lay nothing but heartache, because nothing could ever come of it. They were incompatible in every way but the one.

He was waiting for her in the kitchen, seated at the table looking out of the window at the view of the sea. Because of the way the house was set, most windows would give some view of the sea, Regan realised, if from different angles. It was a perfect location, and must have cost a small fortune for the site alone. For Keir, Australia really had been the land of opportunity.

'That's better,' he commented lightly enough as she dropped into the chair opposite his own. 'You look almost yourself again. Shoulders sore?'

'A little,' she admitted. 'I couldn't stand anything rubbing against them.'

'Hardly surprising. I can feel the heat from here.' He pushed across a platter of cold cuts for her to help herself. 'I'll put you another layer of after-sun on later before you go to bed. I'm afraid you're probably going to peel, though. There are one or two spots on your back that might even blister.'

'I suppose I asked for it,' she said, avoiding his eyes. 'You weren't the only one who told me to cover up. What does Don do for a living?'

The reply came a little short. 'He's a journalist.'

'A good one?'

'Good enough. He's married too, by the way.'

'Separated,' she said 'He told me.'

'You obviously got very chummy. What did you tell him?'

'Nothing important.' This time she made herself look at him directly. 'You do realise what's going to be thought if I stay on here with you?'

His shrug held indifference. 'We could always tell them the truth.'

'And cause even more speculation?' She shook her head, tone bitter. 'We left it too late for that.'

'Then you'll just have to settle for the alternative.' Keir viewed her reaction with cynical eyes. 'It isn't often opportunity knocks twice. I really thought I'd never see you again after I left Cottam. That pride of yours must have taken a real beating this last couple of weeks, but it still won't let go. You couldn't even bring yourself to approach this particular problem with any degree of finesse.'

'You mean properly humbled, ready to beg for the favour?' Her own eyes were stormy. 'You want too much, Keir.'

'There's a difference,' he said, 'between begging and asking, but you wouldn't know it. So pay the other price. You can always tell yourself you're doing it under duress.'

It was on the tip of her tongue to tell him there was no way she was going to let him near her again, but she held it back. There would be time enough to face that aspect when she had to do so. For the present she had a certain immunity. Deliberately she changed the subject, calming her tone.

'This seems too big a house for one man. Wouldn't an apartment have been more convenient?'

If he was disconcerted he didn't show it. His voice when he answered was just as detached as hers. 'I like space around me. Probably because I never had much of it as a boy.'

'But you don't employ any staff?'

'In Sydney? You'd have a hard job finding another Sullivan here. I have a woman come in three times a week to do the rough, the rest I take care of myself.'

'Including the cooking?'

'When I'm not eating out, yes. Nothing elaborate, I'm not a fancy eater. Breakfast is the only time I go to town.'

'I remember.' Regan said it without thinking, feeling her colour rise at the lift of his eyebrow.

'What else do you remember?' he asked softly.

If ever there was a time for letting down her defences it was now, Regan thought with a sudden yearning. What would his reaction be if she told him just how much she did remember—how much he had hurt her? She knew she didn't have that kind of courage. Not while there was every chance that he might find such revelations merely amusing.

'Not a lot,' she said. 'You were hardly with me long enough to leave any lasting impression.'

A spark lit the grey eyes briefly. 'A matter I'll have to rectify this time, one way or another.'

They ate without speaking after that. Regan was thankful to finish, refusing the gateau dessert. Without being asked, she stacked the used dishes in the dishwasher and switched it on, turning back to find Keir had already cleared away the rest of the things they had used with brisk efficiency.

'I'm going outside,' she announced. 'Any objections?'

'None at all.' His tone was as cool as hers. 'You'll need something to cover your shoulders. The temperature drops considerably after dark.'

She went without argument and found the matching cotton stole to her dress, closing the case on the rest of her clothing in the knowledge that she was going to have to unpack some time. It was full dark when she got out to the deck, the stars both brighter and seemingly larger than the ones visible from northerly territories. The breeze coming in off the sea was strong but not chilly.

She drew the stole closer about her, leaning on the rail to gaze out over the darkened pool with a heavy heart. Nothing was going right, and it was chiefly her own fault. Keir was not a man to be coerced into anything. So try another approach, she told herself. Make him see things in a different light. Yes, but how? What could she say that might make him view the situation—or her—with sympathy? She was stuck with her own image.

It was almost an hour before he came to find her, sliding the door from the lounge and speaking through the flyscreen.

'After the overdose of sun you had today you're liable to take a chill standing about out there. Why don't you have an early night?'

'I wouldn't be able to sleep,' she said. 'My body

clock is haywire.' She hadn't turned her head, but her voice carried clearly enough on the night air. 'Do you realise you probably have me to thank for all this?'

There was a pause before the reply came. 'I do?'

'Yes.' She swung round easily, resting both elbows on the rail, her hair lifting about her face in the breeze. 'If I'd married you the first time you'd never have come out here and made your fortune. That means I did you a favour.'

'It's one way of looking at it,' he agreed on a dry note. 'On the other hand, who's to say you wouldn't have come with me?'

'An O'Neil emigrate!' Her laugh was short. 'No chance!'

'You wouldn't have been an O'Neil,' Keir pointed out. 'You'd have been an Anderson. Anyway, wasn't it you yourself told me your great grandfather was Irish? If your grandfather hadn't been granted British citizenship you'd be Irish yourself. By blood you still are. It makes all this "no place like home" business rather meaningless, doesn't it?'

'Not to me it doesn't. I've never even been to Ireland.' Regan forced a shrug, thrusting the subject aside. 'It isn't really important as the question isn't likely to arise. There's only one place I want to be, and that's Cottam!'

He was outside the screens now, his face shadowed by the overhanging roof. 'Supposing you fall in love one of these fine days,' he said with irony, 'and you have to make a choice?'

'I'm not going to fall in love,' she stated flatly. 'I'll never allow my emotions to become involved——' The break off was abrupt; she had almost said 'again', and what Keir would have made of that she hated to think. Deliberately she lightened her voice. 'If I can't find a man I want to have children by I'll adopt a couple. That way everybody's happy. I think I will go in now.'

'Come this way,' he said, and slid open the screen at his side, standing to allow her prior access. She sensed the contempt in his gaze and told herself she didn't care. This was the way he saw her, so this was the way she would be. It was a defence of sorts.

'Drink?' he asked when they were indoors. 'It might help relax you.'

Her hesitation was brief. It was too early to go to bed. Not unless she wanted to spend an hour or two just sitting about twiddling her thumbs. 'Thanks,' she said. 'I'd like a vodka and tonic with a twist of lemon, if you have it.'

He had. Watching him pour the drinks, she thought he would probably have anything she cared to ask for. A surface veneer, he had once called it, but it went deeper than that. The man himself had changed beyond recognition. One would have sworn he had lived this way the whole of his life.

'If you'd anything arranged for tonight, feel free,' she invited, avoiding his eyes as he handed her a glass. 'I'm hardly likely to run away.'

'Not while there's something you want,' he agreed. 'I've nothing specific on, though there's always the chance one or two people might drop in. Life's pretty casual in these parts. Wait around for an invitation and you could wait for ever.'

'You mean all those people this midday just wandered in?'

'In a manner of speaking, although I'd a rough idea how many might make it. The dedicated surfers eat at the beach. Sundays everybody goes to the beach. If you want to swim tomorrow use the pool. I've only seen sharks in the area once while I've been here, but with no spotter to keep an eye open there's always the danger.'

Regan hid a shudder. 'I gather you won't be here.'

'I've business to attend to. I've just been awarded the contract for a whole new hotel and office complex.' The statement was matter-of-fact. 'It's presenting one or two headaches right now.'

'Is that another way of saying you've bitten off more than you can chew?'

Grey eyes narrowed a little. 'It's a way of saying there's a lot of work involved—but I'll be home nights.'

Regan bit her lip, too well aware of his meaning. Useless telling herself discretion was the better part of valour when her tongue kept running away with her. 'I'd have given anything not to have had to come out here,' she said vehemently.

'Nobody was holding a gun to your head,' he pointed out.

Clinking with ice, the glass in her hand felt cold and heavy. She put it down on the nearest available surface and got to her feet, trying not to look as if she were running away. 'I changed my mind. I will have that early night. Sorry about the drink.'

'Don't let it worry you.' Keir sounded unmoved. 'I'll be along in about ten minutes or so with the after-sun.'

There was little point in protesting; it wasn't going to make any difference. She shrugged as if it didn't matter either way, and left him.

She was in bed lying on her face when he did come, the sheet neatly turned down to leave her back and shoulders free. Feeling his weight descend on the edge of the mattress, she clenched her teeth and waited for his ministrations to begin, wanting only to get it over with.

The coolness of the lotion spreading over her burning skin brought instant relief. Despite herself, she felt her body start to relax under the light smoothing strokes of hands normally so powerful, moving inwards from her shoulders to the nape of her neck, then downwards and outwards in smooth concentric motion. Languor stole over her, blanking off her mind from every sensation other than that being inflicted by the long, masculine fingers; stretching her limbs in unconscious sensuality. She wanted those fingers to spread their massage further, to reach every part of her body. Keir's touch had always excited her, even before acquiring this degree of sensitivity. She had never deliberately teased him in the past, simply been incapable of saying no to his caresses. He must have known that then, yet he had never once tried to take things too far. He had loved her as well as wanted her, loved her enough to resist the temptation. If it were only possible to turn back the clock!

She was hardly aware of whispering his name, only of the sudden sense of deprivation when he took his hands away.

'That should help,' he said. 'By morning the heat will have gone out of it. Are you going to sleep like that?'

'Yes.' She had her face half buried in the pillow, fighting the urge to roll over and pull him to her again. 'Thanks for doing this. You've made me quite comfortable.'

His laugh had a brittle quality. 'I'm glad about that. Have a good night. If I'm gone by the time you surface just make yourself at home. I'll be back around five.'

'Fine.' She pretended to be drifting off to sleep, her voice faint and far-away. 'Night.'

He left her without saying anything else, but it was a long time before she did sleep.

As Keir had promised, the fire had gone out of her skin when she awoke at nine, the tension lessened to a degree where she could move quite easily. There was no sound from the rest of the house, no answer to her tentative call. She put on a one-piece swimsuit from her own wardrobe and went out to the pool, but could manage no more than a length in her present condition. In the kind of sticky heat already building, standing water brought little refreshment anyway. The sea was a temptation until one remembered the possibility of sharks. She would be a fool to go against that kind of advice.

There was plenty of food in store. Feeling unusually hungry, Regan scrambled a couple of eggs and made herself some toast and coffee, watching the waves break on the beach some three hundred yards away and wondering what the weather was like back home. She was still sitting there when the back door opened to admit a sturdily built woman in a pair of white Bermuda shorts and red tee-shirt who regarded her without the least surprise.

'It's hot, but!' she announced cheerfully.

'Are you Mrs Anderson?' Regan asked on a cautious note, and saw the other face alter expression.

'Had to go and find himself a Pom, did he?' There was more derision than censure in the remark. 'Always knew going back there'd do him no good. Staying long, are you?'

'You haven't answered my question yet,' Regan pointed out pleasantly. '*Are* you Keir's stepmother?'

The chuckle came deep. 'I'm Betty. Didn't he tell you I come on Mondays?'

'Not exactly. He did mention that someone came in to keep the house in order.'

'That's me.' Her eyes were on the table. 'Is that coffee still hot?'

'It should be,' Regan said. 'I only just made it a few minutes ago.' She hesitated, not quite sure of her ground. 'Betty who?' she asked as the woman got herself a cup from the cupboard and came to pour coffee.

'What? Oh, Milligan. What's yours?'

It was a temptation to tell her exactly who she was

and see her attitude change, but Regan resisted it. 'O'Neil,' she said. 'Regan O'Neil.'

'Sounds like you and my old man might have something in common. His dad came over from Ireland in the thirties. Know any Milligans back there?'

'I'm from the Midlands,' Regan said. 'I've never been to Ireland.'

'It's an Irish name.'

'I know. The family moved to England when my great-grandfather was only a boy. I have a British passport.'

'That's nothing to be so bloody proud of.' The words were tempered by the comparative mildness of the tone. 'Way I hear it, you Poms are having it rough.'

'We've had it rougher,' Regan came back, refusing to rise. 'And I *am* bloody proud of it!' She caught the flash of humour in the other eyes and found herself smiling back. 'Have you been with Mr Anderson very long?'

'About twenty months,' came the easy reply. 'And we don't go in for that Mr business. He's Keir, I'm Betty. Get it?'

'Got it.' Regan came to her feet, pulling the white bathrobe about her. 'Time I was dressed. I suppose you'll be here most of the day?'

'Till twelve. I'm back again on Wednesday.'

'Oh. Well, see you later, then.'

Back in her room, Regan decided to unpack before she did anything else. Not that there was so much to do. She simply hadn't anticipated being here more than a few days at the most. Optimist, she reflected ruefully. Where Keir was concerned she should have known better.

Last night had been his way of showing her exactly who was in control of the situation. And prove it he had. Just five minutes and she had been putty in his hands. He had left her deliberately, of course, just the way he had that first time back at Cottam; using the same technique for maximum effect. Only this time it wasn't going to work; she was determined on that. This time there would be no surrender.

She kept out of Betty's way for the rest of the morning, unwilling to face any further curiosity regarding her presence here. Leaving at twelve, the Australian called a cheerful goodbye from the deck above where Regan was lying stretched out on a lounger beneath one of the umbrellas.

Wednesday was going to bring more problems, unless she arranged to be out for the morning, Regan acknowledged. That shouldn't be too difficult. She could go into town, perhaps take a look at the stores. Keir could hardly expect her to remain in the vicinity of the house for two solid weeks, regardless of how his mind was working. Next week he would be in Brisbane, and she would be free of him. No matter what she had to face from now till then she had that thought to hang on to.

It was too hot to stay outdoors, even in the shade. Regan took a swift dip in tepid water and went to find herself something to eat, blessing the air-conditioning which kept the whole place so beautifully cool and comfortable. On impulse she had a look round the rest of the house while she ate her sandwich, opening doors on a long, low dining room, a book-lined study, a utility containing a complete home laundry and innumerable walk-in closets.

There were three other bedrooms in addition to the one she was using. Decorated in masculine navy with touches of white and gold, Keir's was easy enough to pick out. A double bed, she noted cynically—and wasn't that a stereo set into the headboard? Typical of a bachelor's pad, she supposed, except that he wasn't one any more. She closed the door again abruptly, trying not to think about the women who might have shared that bed with him. If he had meant what he had said last night she would be doing it herself before the week was out.

It was right then that she knew she wasn't going to be able to go through with it. Not for Cottam, not for anything. If that was the price Keir placed on his co-operation then she would tell him to go to hell and stand up to losing the Manor. What was a house anyway compared with one's self-respect? Let it go— start again. It would almost be a relief.

She was dressing after a shower when she heard the car around four-thirty. The blue linen felt cool and fresh as she slid it over her shoulders, refusing to hurry. Let Keir come and find her if he wanted to. Otherwise she would go out to him in her own good time. Whichever way things went, she was moving back to her hotel this evening and he wasn't going to stop her.

Her face in the mirror looked different somehow— or was it just that she could see herself clearly for the first time in ages? Finding a way round her father's dictum had been an obsession with her, excluding every other consideration. Facing up to the fact that she might have to lose Cottam had given her back some sense of integrity, and it showed. She wondered if Keir would see it too.

He seemed to be a long time coming into the house. On impulse Regan went along the corridor to the window at the far end which overlooked the turning circle at the top of the drive. The car was there all right, parked sideways on to her. She could see Keir still in the driving seat, head turned away from her. Only when he moved to open his door did she see that there was someone else in the car with him.

A woman, she realised as the other also got out of the vehicle. A tall, slender woman with dark gold hair drawn back from a face modelled by a sculptor in fine arts. Mid to late twenties at a guess, and no new acquaintance, judging from the way she was smiling at Keir across the roof of the car. Watching, Regan felt something within her tighten up. Who was she? And why had Keir brought her here? Somehow she knew the answer to that question was not one she was going to want to hear.

CHAPTER EIGHT

REGAN was out on the deck when they came, sunglasses hiding her eyes.

'I didn't hear the car,' she said, looking up from the magazine she was ostensibly reading with assumed surprise. 'You said you wouldn't be back before five.'

'It's close enough to that now,' Keir pointed out. 'I'd have thought you'd have had enough sun for a day or two.'

'I haven't been out here long,' she returned with truth. 'Anyway, it isn't as strong at this time of day.' She moved her gaze to the woman at his side, summoning a smile to her lips. 'Hallo.'

The answering smile held a curious quality. 'Hallo.'

'This is Leonie Holt,' said Keir. The pause was brief but meaningful. 'She's going to be staying a while.'

'Really?' Not for anything would Regan have revealed her true state of mind at that moment. 'How nice.'

'She knows the whole story,' he continued inflexibly, 'so you don't have to do any play-acting.' He looked from one to the other, mouth faintly twisted. 'Drink?'

'I'll have a beer,' said Leonie, 'providing it's cold. Last time I was here you were having trouble with the fridge.'

'Faulty unit,' he admitted. 'I had it replaced. Regan?'

'Vodka,' she requested purposely. 'On the rocks.'

Leonie walked to the rail as he went back indoors, leaning her elbows to gaze out over the pool. She was as slim as a reed in the black cord jeans and silky shirt, yet on her the lack of curves looked good.

'Quite a place, isn't it,' she observed. 'You knew Keir designed it himself, of course?'

'No, I didn't,' Regan admitted. 'But that's not surprising. If you know the whole story you might have gathered our relationship doesn't extend itself to casual detail.' She paused there, keeping a tight grip on herself. 'Talking of relationships, do you mind me asking what yours is?'

'Not at all.' The tone was quite unperturbed. 'I'm a friend.'

'A good friend?'

'I like to think so.' Leonie turned her head. 'An understanding one, at any rate. A relationship can exist on more than one level, you know.'

Regan could feel the hardness like an iron band across her chest. For some perhaps, but not for her. 'Just why *are* you here?' she asked, and saw a smile touch the wide mouth.

'I think that's something you'll have to discuss with Keir. I'll make sure you have the opportunity to be alone with him long enough for that.'

'It doesn't have to be a private discussion,' he said from the doorway. 'If we're all going to live together in harmony for the next week or two we'll have everything out in the open where it belongs.'

'I don't agree with you,' Leonie returned pleasantly but firmly. 'And I have to unpack.' She moved towards him, taking her glass from the tray he was carrying with a smile directly into his eyes. 'I'll take this with me. Try not to be too brutal about it.'

Regan couldn't bring herself to meet the grey eyes as he brought across her drink to where she was sitting, despite the dark glasses she still wore. He had a beer himself, the glass chilled opaque. He didn't sit down, standing where Leonie had stood a moment before, his back to the rail, a certain hardness about his face.

'I did some straight thinking after I left you last

night,' he said, 'and I came to the conclusion self-indulgence wasn't going to solve anything for either of us. That's why Leonie is here. To keep us, you might say, on the straight and narrow until I can get you back home.' He was watching her closely, anticipating the reply he saw forming on her lips. 'Don't bother trying to deny it. You wanted me in that bed with you last night, sunburn or no sunburn. You damned nearly got me too. I'm not going to pretend about that. It's a simple matter of chemistry between the two of us—it always has been. Only this time I'm not playing, and neither are you.'

'I didn't ask to stay here,' Regan got out. 'That was entirely your own idea!'

'I know. My baser instincts got the better of me. But not any more. I'll come back with you to sign those papers and that's it. Agreed?'

'Fine.' Pride gave her the control she needed. 'It's all I wanted in the first place. I'll move back to my hotel tonight and you can have your girl-friend all to yourself. That way everyone's happy.'

'You're staying here.' His tone was hard. 'That is if you still want me to make that trip.'

'In other words, you're going to make sure I realise I'm not the only female you ever lusted after. It isn't often a man gets to keep a wife and a mistress in the same house!'

'There's a very good chance,' he said after a long moment, 'that I'm going to finish up beating the hell out of you before you do leave here! Leonie isn't my mistress.'

'A rose by any other name.' The control was slipping bit by bit; she hung on to it grimly. 'Don't expect me to just sit back and take it, Keir. I'm not made that way.'

'Coming from someone who values a pile of old bricks more than her own self-respect, that's almost funny. You put yourself in the way of it, you'd better learn to take it.' He drained the glass and came away from the rail in an abrupt movement. 'I'm going to change. We'll be going out to dinner, by the way.'

'I'm not coming with you.'

He didn't even pause in his advance towards the house. 'That's entirely up to you.'

It was some minutes before Regan could bring herself to move. Her throat hurt with a tight dry pain unrelieved by swallowing. What Keir had said was little more than she had said to herself this afternoon, so why the heartache? She put no value on his good opinion of her; she never had. All he had done was let her off the hook with regard to keeping Cottam. She should be glad about that, not sorry.

Deep down she knew that was only a small part of it. What was really troubling her was far simpler to define. Leonie Holt was not only beautiful, she was nice to go with it. Unusual too to be able to accept the kind of situation presented to her here. A friend, she had said, but the smile which had accompanied that statement had hinted at a more intimate knowledge. To do what she was doing she had to be in love with Keir. There was no other explanation.

And Keir himself? How did he feel? At the time he had married her, there had been no other thought in his mind but the one; certainly none for the future. If he had already been involved with Leonie then he had treated her shabbily, yet she was the one he had appealed to for help in this instance. Because he had realised what she really meant to him? Because he had known her capable of forgiving him anything in her love? A man might well be drawn to a woman like that, not just physically as he was to herself, but emotionally too.

Regan cut off speculation altogether at that point. It was starting to hurt too much.

She was sitting in the living room with the untouched vodka still to hand when Keir came through around seven. He was wearing slacks and a light jacket, his shirt open at the throat.

'Going to change your mind?' he asked.

Regan shook her head, her smile edged with a quite deliberate cynicism. 'Why bother with anything but the truth from now on?' she said. 'Apart from one obvious place, we can't even stand being together. Go on out and enjoy yourself. I'll still be here when you come back. I have to be, don't I, if I want your co-operation.'

'That's right.' His face had hardened again. 'You're going to earn that signature!'

She was doing it already, she thought dully, watching him walk from the room. And at a far greater price than he would ever know.

Leonie did not put in an appearance before leaving. A moment or two later the front door closed and a moment after that Regan heard the sound of the car being started up. The silence after it had gone seemed to close in on her.

If she was going to make a choice now was the time, she acknowledged. All she had to do was pack her things and call for a taxi to take her into town. She could be on a plane winging her way homewards by this time tomorrow. Yes, but to what? came the immediate response. If she went now Keir had won. She couldn't give in so easily. She had come here to save Cottam and save it she would, whatever the cost. It was all she had.

The hours dragged by. When the phone rang at a little after nine she was busy making herself a snack she didn't want, simply for something to do. The receiver was in her hand before she had time to think about it, but once having lifted it she was bound to answer. Her tentative 'Hallo' brought a short silence as if whoever was on the other end had been taken by surprise, then a vaguely familiar male voice returned the greeting with a totally different inflection.

'I was going to ask Keir where you were staying,' went on the man she now recognised as the journalist from the previous afternoon. His laugh held a wry note. 'Seems like maybe he beat me to it. Sorry if I'm barging in, but can I speak to him anyway? Couple of other things I wanted to know.'

'I'm sorry, Don,' Regan kept her voice level. 'He took his other house guest out to dinner. Can I give him any message?'

'Other house guest?' He sounded a little nonplussed. 'You mean he's got two of you staying with him?'

'That's right. Her name is Leonie Holt. Perhaps you know her?'

'No, I don't think so—oh, wait a minute! Does she come from Melbourne?'

'I'm not sure,' Regan hedged. 'I only met her tonight. There wasn't time to talk very much before they went out.'

'You weren't invited?'

'Oh, yes. I just didn't feel like going.' She hesitated before going on, trying to sound casual about it. 'You do know her then.'

'Know of,' he corrected. 'If it's the same one. She's an actress in repertory. Keir goes down to see some of the stuff they put on from time to time.' The pause was speculative. 'You there as chaperone or what?'

Regan's laugh rang false in her ears; she hoped the telephone disguised the fact. 'Hardly a chaperone in this day and age!'

'Oh, I don't know. They've got funny ideas in Melbourne. Real crook place. Anyway, he can't expect to keep two of you to himself. How about making up a foursome tomorrow night?'

'I'm not sure what's planned,' Regan prevaricated.

'That's okay. I'll give Keir a ring in the morning at the office and arrange something. Look forward to it. See you.'

She put down the receiver slowly, not at all sure she had handled that very well. Yet what else could she have said, short of telling the whole story? What else could she be expected to say? If Don kept his promise and rang Keir then he would simply have to deal with the situation the best way he could. She certainly wasn't going to worry about it. She had far too much on her plate already.

She had been in bed almost an hour before she heard the car around eleven; not sleeping, just lying there waiting. They were very quiet coming into the house, voices muted to a low murmur. Regan imagined them going through to the living room, relieved to find her already retired for the night, Keir's offer of a last drink to finish the evening and Leonie's smiling acceptance. He would take both glasses across to where she was sitting and sit down beside her, either on the arm if she was in a chair or the next cushion if she was on a sofa. He might perhaps allow them both a couple of token sips before reaching out to take the glass from her and deposit it with his own out of the way, then he would take her in his arms and kiss her, slowly at first, his lips light and caressing, but gradually increasing their demand until she could no longer hold back any element of response. His hands would be tender with her, not ruthless the way they had so often been with herself, running subtly over that slender body melting against him, rousing her to a pitch where nothing else counted but that he should go on.

There were voices out in the corridor again, so soft they were barely discernible, then a door closed—only one door, Regan noted. She turned over jerkily and pulled the single sheet over her head.

It was raining when she awoke, but though heavy it

didn't last long. The sun was out again and the ground already steaming by the time she was dressed.

Leonie was in the kitchen, a coffee cup almost empty at her elbow. She was wearing shorts and a suntop which made the most of her small but well-formed breasts. The sunglasses pushed up to the top of her head drew back the hair from her face in a fashion only the best of features could take.

'Hi,' she said casually, glancing up from the magazine she was flicking through. 'You must still be suffering from jet-lag.'

Regan could have told her that her tardiness in rising stemmed more from an inability to sleep before the small hours, but she refrained. It gave away too much.

'I've never had to cultivate the habit of early rising,' she said lightly instead. 'Didn't Keir tell you? One of the idle rich, that's me!'

The blue eyes were direct. 'He said you owned a half share in a successful boutique, and worked at it too. That doesn't sound so idle.'

'My, he really gave you a complete potted history, didn't he?' Regan turned from the refrigerator with the glass of orange juice she had just poured and leaned against a nearby unit to view the other girl with what she hoped was the right degree of indifference. 'I suppose he thought you were entitled to know the kind of person he'd married. It must have been quite a shock.'

'It was, but I can understand how it happened.'

'That's very accommodating of you.'

'Isn't it?' Leonie refused to be goaded. 'It isn't all that hard if you think a lot of someone.'

Regan swallowed. 'If you love him so much,' she said thickly, 'why aren't *you* married to him? Or didn't he ever get around to asking you?'

The smile which touched the other mouth seemed oddly out of context. 'I once told him he should lay his ghosts. Not that I expected him to take it quite so literally!'

Regan could not control the run of warmth under her skin. 'Did you enjoy hearing all about it?'

'If you mean what I think you mean,' came the steady reply, 'then I didn't hear anything. I just drew my own conclusions. You don't know him very well, do you? If you did he'd have been the last person you'd have approached with that offer of yours. He should have been anyway, considering the circumstances, but you were probably too arrogant to consider that angle.'

She was right all the way through, Regan acknowledged. Arrogance was the word for it. She kept her expression carefully under control. Preserving her image was her only means of defence.

'It's so much water under the bridge anyway. Providing I get what I want from him in the end I don't give a hoot. You might tell him that.'

'Anything you want him to know you tell him yourself,' Leonie returned without rancour. 'I'm no go-between.'

'All right, I will.' Regan took a grip on herself. 'So what's on the agenda? Do we each go our own way?'

'Not unless you particularly want to. I thought we might take a trip downtown later on, maybe get some lunch while we're out. Keir said you should stay out of the direct sun for a couple of days unless you want real trouble.'

'Nice of him to concern himself!'

Leonie gave a sudden sigh. 'Look, we've got a difficult situation, and you're not making it any easier. Can't we just agree to see him in a different light and leave it at that?'

'Why should I make it easier?' Regan demanded. 'There's no real reason for me to be here at all. He just wants to humiliate me!'

'Perhaps you deserve it.' The smile came suddenly,

robbing the words of some of their sting. 'Just a little.'

She deserved it, full stop, Regan was bound to acknowledge, but admitting it was something else. Her shrug suggested a lack of patience with the whole affair. 'It's not worth discussing. He isn't going to succeed. All right, let's go to town. I'd like the chance to do some shopping while I'm here.'

'Double Bay should answer you prayers—Sydney's a little bit of Paris! A bit pricey, but you get what you pay for. If we leave around ten-thirty we can have a couple of hours before lunch. I'll phone through and book a table at the Summit, if I can get one. You haven't been up the Tower yet?'

'I haven't been anywhere yet,' Regan admitted. 'There's hardly been time.' She tried to stir some enthusiasm. Once she left Australia this time it was extremely unlikely that she would ever come back, so she had better make the most of it. 'I'll be ready,' she said, and drained her glass. 'I'm going to make some toast. Do you want some?'

Leonie shook her head. 'I've already eaten. Is that all you're having?'

'It's all I usually have. Plus coffee, of course.'

'Not much of a combination. How about a steak and a couple of eggs?'

'For *breakfast*?'

'Why not?' There was humour in the blue eyes. 'Put hair on your chest. Alternatively, there's some ham in the fridge. Keir had a couple of slices before he left this morning.'

Regan put bread in the toaster without looking round. 'Did you cook it for him?'

'Yes, I did. He deserves a little pampering now and then. Do you cook at all?'

'On occasion, when I'm in the mood.' Regan shrugged. 'It isn't my favourite pastime.'

'What is?'

'Having a good time. What else?'

Leonie said flatly, 'I don't believe you're as light-weight as you like to make out. Nobody could be. Why the act?'

Regan laughed. 'You're the one who's on the stage.'

There was a brief silence behind her before Leonie spoke again. She sounded odd. 'Who told you that?'

'A friend of Keir's—Don something or other. I never did find out his last name. He rang last night while you were out.'

'Oh?' The odd note was still there. 'I didn't realise any of Keir's friends knew me.'

'He doesn't. He said he'd heard Keir mention your name.' Regan paused. 'You've been here before, though, haven't you?'

'Only once, and very fleetingly. I didn't get around to meeting anybody.' Leonie's tone lightened again, almost deliberately. 'Maybe Keir will do something about it this time.'

'Mightn't that create some difficulties, considering the set-up?'

'I don't see why it should. So far as the outside world is concerned we're just house guests. They'll probably think he got his dates mixed up.'

Regan doubted it. No one who knew Keir would believe him capable of that kind of error. Yet did it really matter all that much what people thought? Let them speculate. She would be gone in a couple of weeks.

For the first time she found herself contemplating that long journey home with Keir at her side, and felt her throat close up. If she had realised at the time just what she was going to have to go through in order to persuade him to return with her she would never have come. This way she was going to be deserted not once but twice by the man she had married.

Her voice came out harsher than she had intended.

'You do realise it's going to be at least a couple of years before he'll be free to marry you? Are you willing to wait for him that long?'

Leonie took her time answering, face reflecting a certain indecision. 'My feelings for Keir don't come with any strings attached,' she said at last. 'If he needs me I'm available. That's all there is to it.' She pushed back her chair and got up, the movement fluid. 'I'm going to change. I'll order a taxi to take us down town. Are you sure half ten is going to give you enough time?'

'Quite sure.' Regan bit into the slice of toast she didn't feel in the least like eating, swallowed dryly and added, 'It will only take me a few minutes to change. You go along.'

Left alone at last she thought about what Leonie had just said. In all probability the Australian girl would move in here permanently as soon as she was gone. When the time came they might marry or they might not. It didn't appear to be of very great importance to Leonie. For her love was enough.

Leonie proved to be an excellent guide when it came to shopping, taking her from the boutiques of Double Bay to the big department stores like Myers and Grace Brothers where goods from all over the world were on display. Regan bought one or two smaller items, plus a pair of very expensive thonged sandals which happened to take her fancy, but could conjure little real interest in adding to her wardrobe. Any garment bought here would only serve as a reminder every time it was worn, and that was something she wasn't going to need.

The view from the revolving Tower restaurant was magnificent: the harbour busy with all kinds of craft through from sailboats to super-tankers, the green spread of the Botanic Gardens around the curve of Farm Cove; the open sea lying put there beyond the Heads for thousands of uninterrupted miles. Seen from this height downtown Sydney had canyons for streets, the traffic moving as if controlled from a central source like some gigantic toytown layout. The bridge came into view again as they finished their meal, completing the two-hour revolution.

'We could take a boat trip out on the harbour next time we come in,' Leonie suggested when they had dragged themselves away from the window table. 'Sydneysiders always say you haven't seen it at all till you've seen it from the water.'

'There's plenty of time,' Regan pointed out. 'What's wrong with now?'

'We have to go and see Keir at the office. Pick up the keys to the car.'

'Car?'

'He thought we needed transport of our own stuck out there at North Beach. I told him we'd collect it while we were downtown. It's only a couple of blocks to his office.' A smile crossed her face. 'And about seventeen floors straight up! We'll have to get him to take us out to the factory some time. He's just expanded again. The way things are he's going to need further premises. Everybody's interested in staying cool, especially if they can do it at a reasonable cost. By all accounts, the European sales are already well up.'

Regan said softly, 'You seem to know a lot about it.'

'Only as much as Keir tells me from time to time. In that respect he's right on the general Aussie wavelength—when not at work forget it. We value our leisure time more than most.' Leonie moved forward as the elevator slowed to a stop. 'Back to earth! Come on.'

Regan followed her with mixed feelings, curious to see Keir's place of business yet reluctant to face him again before she absolutely had to. Last night he had slept with Leonie, knowing she herself was only mere feet away. If he had done it purposely to show her how little their own shared experiences had meant to him, then he had succeeded. What she doubted was her ability to look him in the eye and pretend it didn't matter to her.

Trapped by the buildings all around, the heat outside was a tangible force, the blue sky above a reflecting mirror for the merciless sun. Regan for one was thankful to reach their destination, following Leonie into yet another dim, cool elevator to swoop swiftly upwards.

Keir's office turned out to be on the sixteenth, not the seventeenth floor. His secretary was a woman in her thirties, cheerful and efficient and obviously expecting them.

'He's got an appointment at three,' she advised. 'That gives you twenty minutes in there, no more.'

'We'll be out in ten,' Leonie promised. 'Can we go straight through?'

'I'd better tell him you're here,' said the other woman. 'He's been out of sorts most of the day for some reason. Not like him.' She flicked the intercom switch and spoke briskly into it. 'Your visitors are here. Do I send them in?'

'Yes.' The single word sounded clipped. 'And where's that letter I asked for?'

'Still looking. Must have got misfiled.' She lifted her eyebrows in comical appeal to the two girls facing her across the desk as she released the switch. 'See what I mean? Go on in—and the best of luck!'

Keir was standing at the big window looking out over the downtown area when they entered the room. His desk was set at right angles to it, the swivel chair pushed back as if he had just risen to his feet. He was wearing a tie today, Regan saw as he turned towards them, but it was loosened at the neck, the shirt button beneath unfastened. The smile he summoned was perfunctory.

'I don't have much time,' he said, 'so let's keep this

short. The car's a blue Packard parked next to mine in the lot. The gateman will show you where.' He moved back to the desk to pick up a key ring, handing it to Leonie who was nearest. 'The tank's full, and it's insured for you both to drive.'

'Providing it isn't together,' quipped Regan, determined to keep up the part she had given herself to play. 'You didn't have to bother. If I wanted to drive around I'd hire my own.'

'You can still do that,' he returned in the same taut vein. 'Nobody's stopping you.'

She forced herself to meet the hard regard without flinching. 'It would be easier all round if I simply moved back to town, wouldn't it?'

'I've already told you that isn't on.'

'You mean you haven't had your full pound of flesh yet?' Her smile matched the shrug. 'Mustn't rob you of *that* pleasure, must I?'

Leonie moved sharply. 'I think we'd better be going before somebody says something they're going to regret.'

'A good idea.' Keir was in control of himself, but with an expression in his eyes that boded ill for any further exchange. 'Incidentally, we're all going out to dinner tonight—and I mean all. Invitation from Don Crossman. He suggested that new place out at Palm Beach, so he'll be picking us up at the house. Not much point in using two cars.' He was still looking at Regan, registering her response with a curl of his lip. 'No surprise to you, of course. He told me he spoke to you last night. Just remember he's a journalist first and foremost. If he can get a story he won't be too particular how he uses it.'

'He probably thinks you're starting a harem,' she said. 'I'll do my best to disillusion him. Hot romance and air-conditioning don't really go together, do they.'

'We're leaving,' put in Leonie with haste. 'See you later, Keir.'

Regan accompanied her without protest, too well aware of the thin line she was treading. Goading Keir like that did nobody any good, yet she couldn't seem to stop herself. She wanted to hurt him, the way he had hurt her—the way he was still hurting her. Words were the only weapon she had.

They had the lift to themselves going down. Leonie was the first to speak.

'One of these days you're going to go too far,' she said bluntly. 'I've never seen Keir lose his temper, but I don't imagine he can't. All right, so he's as much to blame for accepting that offer as you are for making it, but at least he's willing to make some amends by coming back to England with you.'

Regan was studying their twin reflections in the mirrored wall: same height, same skin tone, almost the same shaped face; only the hair essentially different. 'At a price,' she said.

'So he's human. Not that I necessarily think he's right about that either.'

'Only if that's the way he wants it you'll go along.'

'More or less. It's what——' They were stopping; Leonie cut off the rest, biting her lip. 'Let's go and find that car.'

They were in it and heading across the bridge before she spoke again, this time on a harder note.

'One thing you should know—Keir and I haven't slept together. Does that make things easier?'

It might if she didn't know better, Regan thought wearily. She knew what Leonie was trying to find out, and she had no intention of giving herself away. 'I honestly couldn't care less,' she said. 'He doesn't belong to me. All I do care about is getting out of that house!'

'Well, I doubt if you're going to. Not if you want

him to do what you're asking. Like you say, he's set his price. I'd say it was small enough, considering it's only your pride that's at stake.'

'I don't understand you,' Regan confessed after a moment or two. 'You do know *why* he brought you into the act?'

The fleeting smile was totally at odds with the answer. 'Because he finds you very hard to resist even now? Yes, he told me that much. You should think yourself lucky he didn't decide to indulge his feelings as part of the price. Not that I imagine it would have been such a dreadful penalty to pay.'

She sounded so convincing. Could she possibly be telling the truth? Regan thought back to the previous night, trying to convince herself. She had heard one door close, true, but who was to say there hadn't been another after she had buried her head in the pillow? On the other hand, what real difference did it make in the long run? Leonie was staying in the house at Keir's invitation. Whether they slept together or not was purely incidental.

'If we're going to talk at all can we change the subject?' she said abruptly. 'I'm tired of this one. You're with a repertory company, aren't you? Fortnightly or weekly?'

'Weekly. The theatre closed for six weeks,' Leonie added, anticipating the next question. 'Structural alterations. We'll have a new stage when we reopen, though we'll be minus a row of seats out front.'

'That doesn't sound such good policy.'

'It mightn't be if we normally played to full houses. This way there'll be fewer empty ones and a better standard of production to keep it that way, we hope.' There was animation in her voice. 'We run into a lot of competition from other theatre groups, so it's very much a case of who can put on the best drawing programme. Do you like live theatre yourself?'

'Very much,' Regan admitted. 'We don't have a professional group in Cottam, but we do have an excellent amateur company.'

'I suppose you go to London when you want the real thing.'

'Not as often as I used to. I saw every Broadway play worth seeing in November, though.'

'Really?' Leonie laughed. 'Now you've really got me envious! Tell me about New York. I've always wanted to visit the States.'

They were still deep in conversation when they reached the house. Only as Leonie brought the car to a standstill at the top of the drive did Regan come back reluctantly to the reality of the situation, aware of some confusion of mind. Wrapped up as the other girl was in the theatre, where did Keir fit into her life?

'If you had to give it up,' she said, 'would you be able to?'

The reply seemed a long time in coming. Leonie faced front, her hands still on the wheel, face blank of expression. 'If I had to choose,' she said at last, 'yes, I would.' She opened the car door before Regan could say anything else. 'I'm going for a dip. Coming?'

Regan followed her more slowly, feeling depressed. She wished it were only possible to compress these days of waiting. She wanted badly to go home.

She was in her room ostensibly resting when she heard Keir arrive home around six. Leonie greeted him in the hallway, her voice just audible through the partially opened bedroom door.

'Regan's asleep,' she said, and paused before adding on a different note, 'Do you really think tonight is such a good idea?'

It was impossible to hear Keir's reply because of the lower pitch and lack of projection, but the inflection was curt.

'I don't think she'd do that,' Leonie said in answer.

'She must be as reluctant as you are to have it made public. Come and have a beer out on the deck. We've plenty of time.'

Regan lay still on the bed as their footsteps faded away, eyes fixed on the ceiling. So Keir believed she had put Don up to inviting them all out tonight. At least, that was what it had sounded like. What motive he thought she might have in mind she wasn't at all certain, but there was one she could easily provide.

CHAPTER NINE

SHE chose a creamy silk pants suit for the evening, leaving the jacket open to show the shaped opera-top bodice and sliding her feet into flimsy sandals. Her skin was already turning brown, she noted with some satisfaction, the threatened peeling confined to a tiny area at present hidden. The grey eyes gazing back at her from the mirror gave no clue to the thoughts behind them. She looked serene and confident and totally unaffected by emotional cross-currents. All she had to do was hold that pose.

She deliberately waited until Don had arrived before going through to join the party in the living room. Both men were informally dressed in slacks and jackets and open-necked shirts, but like herself, Leonie had opted for an intermediate style in the shape of an apricot dress in a fine Italian knit cotton which suited her slender figure admirably.

'I'm not surprised you tried to keep 'em to yourself, mate,' commented Don dryly to Keir. 'I'd have done the same.'

The lightness of the answering shrug was belied by the hardness in the grey eyes. 'A man can but try. Would you like a drink before we go, Regan?'

She shook her head, seeing that the others had almost finished their own. 'I'll wait until we get there, thanks. Is it far?'

'About thirty kilometres,' Don told her. 'It'll be dark before we get there, but I'm told we can't miss it. I only hope it turns out to be as good as it's supposed to be.'

'If it isn't,' said Regan, smiling at him, 'you'll have

to do this all over again to make up for it. Just think about that!'

'I am.' He was smiling back, apparently oblivious to the others in the room. 'Just don't expect Savoy standards.'

'You've been to England?' she queried.

'A couple of times. Not that I stayed at the Savoy. Holiday Inn was more to my pocket.' His glance encompassed the two listening to the exchange. 'We'd better get moving or they might let the table go. There's a group for dancing on Tuesdays.'

Seating arrangements in the car seemed to be taken for granted, both girls being relegated to the rear seat. Not her choice either, Leonie's look of tolerant resignation said, but what could they do about it? There was little conversation between the two of them during the drive, nor if it came to that between the two men. Once or twice Regan caught Don's eye on her through the driving mirror and knew she was in for some pertinent questions the moment he had her alone. It would be interesting to find out what she was going to say when that time came, because right now she had no idea. Neither did she care very much.

Silvers turned out to be a large converted old house set in its own grounds on the south side of Palm Beach. Regan found the ground-floor restaurant overcrowded and noisy, but the food was good, the wines excellent, so she was able to answer with a fair degree of truth when Don asked her what she thought of the place.

'Today at lunch was the first time I'd ever tasted Australian wine,' she confessed. 'I hope you won't take it the wrong way if I say I didn't expect to find it so palatable.'

'You're not on your own,' he responded, 'but the word's spreading.' He nodded towards the small, packed dance area. 'Feel like being elbowed to death?'

Regan avoided looking in Keir's direction. 'I'll risk it.'

Of necessity he drew her close once they were on the floor, hands sliding about her back. 'I'm not sure this idea's going to work,' he commented close by her ear. 'Not enough room. They'd do better sticking in a few more tables and settling for music.'

'They might still do that,' Regan said lightly, knowing they were both of them making small talk for the sake of it. 'Judging by the number of people here they'd certainly fill them.'

'Always supposing they'd still want to come if there wasn't any dancing.' He was smiling as he said it; she could hear it in his voice. His next words confirmed it. 'So much for the irrelevant detail. I think I've worked a couple of things out.'

Her voice was creditably level. 'About what?'

'The reason you and Leonie are both staying at his place.' He didn't wait for any comment on her part. 'You surprised him by turning up out of the blue and he needed a third party around to keep it light. Near enough?'

Regan wanted suddenly to laugh. So near and yet so far! 'You said a couple of things,' she reminded him, purposely not answering the question.

'That may have been a bit premature. I think you came out to Aussie specifically to see Keir, but I'm not all that sure why.'

'A broken heart?' she suggested on a note of irony, and drew a laugh.

'Not you! You're not the type. More like a demand you resented having to make—at least that's the impression you gave on Sunday.'

She was shaken by his perception but not about to reveal it. 'Top marks for observation.'

He waited a moment or two before saying softly, 'Is that all you're going to tell me?'

'I haven't told you anything,' she pointed out. 'It's all guesswork on your part.'

'But you haven't denied it.'

'I don't see the need.'

Don gave a sudden sigh of half-humorous resignation. 'This isn't professional curiosity. I'm not into social gossip. Right now I'm not even employed on a regular basis. I'm taking a six-month sabbatical to try my hand at writing the book everybody's supposed to have in them.'

'And you're running out of material?' Regan wanted to bite back the words the moment she had said them. She put a swift, penitent hand to the side of his face. 'I'm sorry, that was uncalled for.'

'Not so much,' he admitted. 'I sensed a story the minute I saw you and Keir together. You're a long way from being friends, yet there's something in the way you look at one another——' He paused briefly. 'You're not in any kind of trouble, are you?'

Her laugh was brittle. 'Not the kind you mean. Stop fishing, Don.'

'I want to help, that's all.'

'Why?' she asked bluntly. 'You barely know me.'

'So what the hell!' He held her away from him to look at her, eyes angry. 'Can't you take anything at face value?'

'Apparently not.' She studied him a moment, aware that his tanned, attractive features did nothing to her heartstrings. Her smile had a rueful quality. 'I'm not a child, Don, I can sort out my own problems. Thanks all the same.'

'Okay, forget it.' He sounded rueful himself. 'How long are you staying?'

'A week or so.'

'Until Keir gets back from Brisbane?'

Further prevarication was a waste of time, Regan decided. He would find out soon enough. 'Yes,' she said.

'Then that gives you all next week on your own. All I want to say is you don't have to be. Nothing heavy. I'd just like to see you.'

It was the first time Regan had allowed herself to think that far ahead. Now she realised that what Don said was true. With Keir out of the way there would be no further need for Leonie to stay on at the house. No reason why she should either. She could move back downtown to await his return, spend some time seeing the sights on her own. The thought had little appeal. Nothing heavy, Don had said, and she believed him. He too had had enough of emotional entanglement. They would be company for one another, that was all.

'If you let me have your phone number,' she said, 'I could give you a ring. I'm not quite sure what my plans are. Do you mind if we sit the rest of this out? You were right about being elbowed to death.'

The other two had not danced. Keir watched them coming with an enigmatic expression, his hand lying close enough to Leonie's on the white cloth to have been holding it but a moment before.

'Sorry to break up the evening so early,' he announced, 'but Leonie has a bad head. Pity we all came in the one car.'

It would probably have been simple enough to order a taxi, but Don refrained from making the point. 'That's okay,' he said. 'It's not what I expected either. I'll see you out at the car after I've paid the bill.'

Keir walked between the two girls as they went outside, but touching neither. His face looked austere in the moonlight, his mouth an uncompromising line. He unlocked the car with the keys Don had given him and saw the two of them into the rear seat, moving forward to slide into the front passenger seat himself.

'How does your head feel now?' asked Regan without looking in Leonie's direction. 'Better, I hope.'

It was Keir who answered, voice brusque. 'She

doesn't have a headache, as you very well know. I wanted out.'

'And what you want you have to have, of course.'

'Don's coming,' put in Leonie hastily as Keir half turned in his seat. 'He's going to wonder what's going on if he gets in here in this atmosphere!'

'Perhaps he won't need to wonder,' said Regan with deliberation. 'Very acute, is our friend Don. What he doesn't know, he guesses.'

There was no time for more because Don was opening the driver's door. Keir subsided back into his own seat, face cold and hard. The reckoning would come later, there was no doubting that. She had goaded him once too often. But at that particular moment Regan couldn't bring herself to care very much. She felt tired and dispirited and more than ready to throw in the towel.

Despite the early break-up of the evening, it was gone ten-thirty by the time they reached the house. Don declined Keir's invitation to call in for a nightcap, keeping the engine running as they all got out of the car.

'Don't forget Sunday,' he said through the wound-down window. 'I'll let you know which beach we're using after we hear the surf forecasts. You owe me the chance to get even, mate.'

'You'll get it,' Keir promised. 'Thanks for the dinner.'

'Yeah, well, the food wasn't bad.' He lifted a hand in farewell to all three of them standing there on the driveway. 'See you!'

Leonie was the first to move. 'I'm going to bed,' she announced. 'That headache came on for real while we were driving back. Anyway, I'd rather not be around while you two sort things out.'

'So far as I'm concerned there's nothing to sort out,' Regan said levelly. 'Why don't we all call it a day?'

'Because there are one or two things I have to say, whether you feel like listening or not,' put in Keir on a determined note. 'Leonie, are you going to be all right? Can I get you anything?'

The golden head moved in negative response. 'It isn't that bad.' She hesitated, her glance flicking to Regan's face, then back again. 'Can I speak to you for a moment?'

'Don't mind me,' Regan assured her, and moved on ahead of them into the house. 'I'll be in the living room,' she tossed over a shoulder.

The place was in darkness. She put on a couple of lamps and stood waiting in the middle of the room, knowing she would be at a disadvantage if she sat down. This whole situation was becoming more than she could bear, and she was sure Leonie felt the same. Whatever satisfaction Keir might gain from making her stick it out, he surely had to realise that Leonie was being humiliated too. It was probably what she was pointing out to him right now, though whether it would do any good remained open to doubt. He was concerned only with his own feelings.

He came in after a few minutes, attitude not visibly altered. 'How much did you tell Don?' he demanded without preamble.

'Not a thing,' she returned. 'I didn't have to. He put two and two together and came up with his own story.' Her smile held a mockery as much self-directed as anything. 'He thought I might be pregnant by you, and here to claim certain rights—marriage, I imagine, being one of them. You don't need to worry. I convinced him it wasn't true. Of course, I had to half promise to spend some time with him next week in order to do it.'

'You won't be here next week,' Keir stated flatly. 'I've altered my schedule. I'm flying up to Brisbane in the morning, back in Sydney by Saturday. Monday we leave for England.'

Regan gazed at him without speaking for several long seconds, emotions suddenly numbed. 'Why?' she got out at last. 'Why did you change your mind?'

The reply came clipped, every word a hammer blow. 'Because I want you out of my hair as soon as possible.'

Ludicrously her eyes went to it, thick and dark, the memory of how it felt to run her fingers through it overwhelmingly real. So she had got her own way after all. He had given in. But she knew that wasn't wholly true. What he was doing he was doing for Leonie.

'I know the feeling,' she said, and made no effort to keep the bitterness from her voice. 'I'll be packed and ready. Now do you mind if I go to bed?'

Eyes like steel, Keir moved out of line with the doorway. 'Go ahead.'

Alone in her room, she didn't bother to put on a light, standing there motionless in the darkness as she bleakly considered the future. By this time next week she would be back at Cottam and safely in ownership—and it meant nothing to her. It was Keir she wanted, not a pile of old bricks; Keir she loved, regardless of all that had passed between them. Had there ever been a time, she wondered, when she had stood a chance of reawakening that same emotion in him? Had she come here in open acknowledgement of her need to be with him would they have found some level of communication? She would never know. It was too late—much, much too late.

The night was long, sleep when it came fitful and disturbed. Awakening at three, Regan lay for some time trying to recapture that elusive state of forgetfulness, but with little hope. In a few hours Keir would be gone, leaving her with four whole days to get through before his return. What would she do? How would she spend them? Not with Don Crossman, for

certain. He was too capable of seeing through her. So was
Leonie, if it came to that, yet if the other girl stayed on
there was going to be no avoiding her.

The obvious alternative was to leave herself—to
return home to England tomorrow or the next day and
let Cottam go. And have Keir guess why, a small voice
whispered. No, that wasn't the answer either. He must
never know how she felt about him. That way she at
least retained some degree of pride.

She got up eventually, unable to bear the endless
circling of her mind a moment longer. The house was
silent, the sound of the sea breaking on to the beach
loud in her ears. On impulse she donned a thin wrap
over her nightdress and went out to the deck, moving
quietly in order not to disturb the other inmates. It
was cool outside in contrast to the heat of the day, but
pleasantly so, the north-easterly wind curling tendrils
of hair about her face. In the bright light of the moon,
the beach had a silvery glitter, the sea beyond stretching to infinity. Eleven thousand miles from home, and
it felt like a million. It might as well be a million for all
the difference it made.

The grass was soft beneath her bare feet, like velvet.
Queensland blue, Keir had called it. A low fence was
all that separated garden from beach, a gap sufficing
for a gateway. Regan walked out across the sand, feeling the grains oozing between her toes and out again,
smelling the salty tang on the wind. She stopped just
short of the breaking waves, watching the curl of white
foam just beginning to break along the crest of another
a few yards out. Not a surfing beach, they had said,
yet the waves were longer and deeper than any she had
ever seen back home—something to do with the distance they travelled between forming and breaking, she
imagined. The longer the run the greater the enjoyment.

She had lost track of how long she had been standing

there when she first became aware that she was no longer alone. When she turned her head, Keir was mere feet away, hands thrust deep into the pockets of his slacks as he contemplated her.

'Thinking of taking a dip?' he asked with irony. 'Or were you just sleepwalking?'

'I couldn't sleep.' Her tone was brusque. 'That's why I'm down here. 'I'm sorry if I woke you, but you didn't have to follow me.'

'I wasn't asleep either,' he said. 'And I wasn't sure what you had in mind.'

She forced a laugh, short and derisive. 'I wasn't thinking of ending it all, if that's what you imagined. My balance of mind is quite undisturbed.'

His eyes glittered suddenly and dangerously. 'Is it? Can you look me in the face and tell me you've got everything you want in life right at this moment?'

'No,' she admitted. 'But I will have once I have your signature where it's needed.' She met his gaze without flinching, her own eyes totally expressionless. 'You wouldn't understand how I feel about Cottam. To you a house is just somewhere to live. You designed this one here, but I doubt if it really means anything to you.'

'It comes pretty far down my list of priorities,' Keir agreed. 'It's the people who live in a place that makes it special, not the other way round. Cottam will never be what it was in your great-grandfather's day, no matter how many husbands you try on for size. No modern family would fill it the way it should be filled.'

In turning towards him Regan had faced directly into the warm wind angling in from the sea. She put up a hand to smooth back the hair blowing across her face, oblivious to the manner in which the thin wrap was moulding itself to her body. 'So what would you suggest? That I have it bulldozed to make way for so-called progress?'

'Not a bit. I'd turn it into a convalescent home, or something similar. It's ideally situated. Or how about a health farm? A little capital outlay and you'd be well on the way to making another fortune. There'd even be a job for Sullivan if he wanted it. Imagine the prestige he'd lend the place!'

'Shut up!' Regan snapped fiercely. 'I don't want to hear any more!'

'Because you know I'm making the only sense.' He moved without warning, taking her by the shoulders with a roughness that jerked back her head, looking down into her stormy face with grim intent. 'No matter how much money your father left you, that house is going to take more and more of it! Can't you see that far ahead?'

Her pulses were racing, her whole body alive to his touch, to his closeness. She had to get away, she thought wildly, before she gave herself away—before she lost control and begged him to keep her here with him. She could stand to lose him better than she could stand his pity.

'Hadn't you better get back before your mistress misses you?' she flung at him. 'The bed will be getting cold!'

The blaze springing alight in the grey eyes was swift and frightening. Instinctively she pulled away from him, spinning on her heel as she did so to run from him along the beach, panic lending her wings. With the sand deadening all sound, she couldn't be sure how close he was behind her, and didn't dare pause to find out. That he would be behind her she had no doubt. The anger in him had to have outlet.

She was sobbing for breath when he finally caught her, too far gone to fight him as he pulled her roughly about to face him. His jaw was clamped rigid, his skin around his mouth showing white under the pressure. His hands were like steel.

'I warned you,' he gritted. 'You damned little——'

She hit him then, striking out blindly at the lean brown cheek, seeing the fury in him change character as her fingers connected. Then she was down in the sand with his full weight on top of her, his mouth covering hers with a savagery that allowed her no quarter, hurting her yet not hurting her, because it was what she wanted too, this hard, fierce passion overriding everything else.

Her response was sudden and abandoned, her hands curving his back to draw him closer, her body softening to sensuality beneath him. She felt the anger drain away, his mouth lose its hardness, the touch of his fingers like fire on her skin. When they came together it was as if they had never been apart.

Keir was the first to regain control of himself, moving away abruptly to sit up and adjust his clothing.

'I'm not going to make any excuses,' he said without turning his head. 'You had that coming.'

'We both had it coming.' Her voice sounded thick in her ears. 'Wasn't that why you sent for Leonie?'

'For what good it did.' He ran a hand through his hair, the movement rough. 'I should have settled for what was on offer and left it at that. Anyway, it's immaterial now.'

'Not to me it isn't,' Regan wanted to say, but the words wouldn't come. It had been purely physical for him, he couldn't have made that plainer. It changed nothing at all.

Pulling the thin cotton wrap about her, she pressed herself to her feet, registering the weakness in her limbs without surprise. There was sand in her hair, in her eyes, even in her mouth. 'I shan't tell her about tonight, if that's what's worrying you,' she said huskily. 'I'm not too proud of it myself. Do you mind giving me five minutes to get to the house before you follow me? Right now I'm not sure I can bear you near me.'

'Sure.' He sounded tired. 'You'll get over it.'

Regan could hear the sound of a vacuum cleaner some-where in the house when she awoke next morning. Memory brought depression, instant and deep. She kicked off the sheet hurriedly and got up, eager for action of any kind which would keep her mind occupied. Dwelling on things never did any good, but forgetting had to be worked at. By the time Keir came back she had to be able to look him in the eye without emotionalism rearing its head.

Leonie was in the pool, slim body cutting the water like a knife. Reluctant to come up against Betty again, Regan went down to join her, taking a seat beneath one of the umbrellas to watch the other complete a dozen lengths. She would have gone in herself had she been able to stir up enough energy. The humidity lay like a pall.

'Are you escaping the inquisition too?' asked Leonie when she finally came out. 'Talk about curiosity killing the cat! I gather you met our friend in there on Monday.'

'Yes, I did.' Regan waited a moment before putting the question. 'What did you tell her?'

'Nothing she believed.' The smile came faint. 'She probably thinks he cut out because he couldn't take the pace any longer.'

Regan kept her voice level. 'He did get off all right, then?'

'First thing. From the look of him I don't think he'd slept all that well. He told you he'd be back here by Saturday?'

'Yes.' Regan hesitated, not at all certain how to put it. 'Are you planning on staying till then?'

'No, I'll be leaving this afternoon.' Leonie had thrown herself down on the next lounger, long, slender legs stretched, eyes half closed against the light filtering through the material above. 'I'm meeting my husband off the L.A. flight in the morning, so I need to be back in Melbourne tonight.'

'Your husband?' Regan's voice seemed to be coming from a long way off. 'I—I don't understand.'

'It's simple enough. Keir knew Jimmy was away on business and that the theatre was closed. When he explained the situation here I offered to help out any way I could.'

'But I thought—You told me——' Regan broke off, trying to remember just what had been said. Could she have interpreted the whole thing wrong from the start?

'That was my own idea,' Leonie confessed, turning her head with a rueful expression. 'Keir would be furious if he knew what I'd been up to. You see, I didn't really believe it when he told me you'd come all this way just to get him to sign some papers. I believed it even less when I saw the two of you together. I thought if I roused your jealousy a little you might just decide to show your real feelings.'

Regan stared at her, scarcely able to take it in. 'You mean you only pretended to be interested in him?'

'I didn't have to pretend the interest. He and Jimmy have been friends for years, and since I married Jimmy it's been a three-way thing. He comes down to Melbourne every month to catch a performance.'

'But you said you loved him.'

'So I do. Next to Jimmy he's the finest man I know. The only way I really lied was in letting you think I was only waiting for him to unload you before grabbing him for myself. Even then I made a point of emphasising that we'd never slept together, if you remember.'

'I remember.' Regan spoke slowly, the initial buoyancy of spirit already fading. It made little difference in the long run; last night had made that clear. She could rouse Keir to physical passion but that was as far as it went. 'Well, thanks for making the effort,' she got out, 'but you really were wasting your time. All I want from him is that signature, then I'll be more than happy to leave him alone.'

'Signature to what exactly?' asked Leonie on a curious note. 'Keir seemed so hazy about it himself.'

'I haven't seen the paper in black and white,' Regan was forced to admit.

There was a lengthy pause before Leonie spoke again, voice soft. 'Are you sure you didn't dream up the whole idea just to get Keir back to England with you?'

'No, I didn't!' Regan had stiffened. 'It was my solicitor who said he had to come back, and he must know what he's talking about.'

'I suppose so.' The concession was made with reluctance. 'But I still think you're kidding yourself over the way you feel about Keir. Did you ever stop to wonder why you'd choose a man like him for something like this in the first place?'

'He just happened to put in an appearance at the right moment.'

'A man you'd once turned down. Hardly an ideal candidate, was he?'

Regan shrugged, fighting to maintain her equilibrium. 'I was getting too close to the deadline to worry about things like that.'

'And that's the part that doesn't jell. If you were half as calculating as you make out, you'd have had some businesslike arrangement already worked out, with all the legal detail tied up *before* the marriage, not after. I think you probably lost your head when you saw Keir again and plunged in blindly, hoping everything would eventually come right. It might have done too if he'd stayed around long enough.'

'You couldn't be more wrong,' Regan said jerkily. 'I made an error of judgment, that's all. Now can we forget the whole subject, please?'

Leonie sighed. 'If that's the way you want it. But I think you're being a fool. You could have had Keir eating out of the palm of your hand if you'd gone about it the right way. You probably still could.'

She subsided then, leaving Regan free to cautiously explore the innermost recesses of her mind. Could it possibly be true what Leonie had said? Had she made Keir that offer in the deep-down hope that he would refuse to accept his dismissal from her life again once they were married? She remembered that first moment of seeing him again, the emotions he had awoken in her. No other man had ever made her feel that same vital awareness, that was certainly sure. The lack of it was the main reason she had kept Robin dangling for so long.

Yet supposing Leonie was right in her assessment? It didn't help her now. Keir wanted only to be rid of her.

CHAPTER TEN

THE house seemed so quiet after Leonie had gone that afternoon. Listening to the creaking of the ceiling joists as they expanded in the heat, Regan knew she couldn't stand the thought of another three days like this. Whether Keir liked it or not she had to move to a hotel.

She was packed and ready to go by the time the taxi she had phoned for arrived. She left a note explaining where she had gone in a prominent position in the kitchen, and took the house keys with her, knowing Keir had his own. Betty would be in for another surprise if she turned up on Friday, but no doubt she would take it in her stride.

There was another of the sudden heavy downpours on the way into town, eliciting a curse from her driver when his windscreen wipers failed to work. They had to sit it out at the roadside until the rain stopped, most of which time they spent talking about 'back home'. He had come from Wolverhampton three years previously, Regan discovered, and obviously still suffered from occasional homesickness. He wanted to know everything, right down to the price of coal—which she couldn't tell him.

'Times when I've thought about going back,' he admitted at one point. 'But then I look round at what I've got here and think what the hell for? We're buying our own home, the kids are at a good school, we've got a bit of money in the bank, and with thirty miles of beaches right on the doorstep we don't need to go off on annual holiday. Then there's the weather. You know, there's hardly a weekend out of the whole year that we can't get off outdoors. Took the kids to Lake Macquarie for a few days this last winter. Real bonza place!' His grin seemed to acknowledge a deliberate use of the Australian slang term. 'There's only the wife can't water-ski now, and that's only because she likes to drive the boat. Hated the water back home, she did. Always used to complain it was too cold.'

'What about things like sharks and snakes?' Regan asked. 'Aren't you scared that the children might get hurt?'

'They're not likely to if we use some common sense,' the man came back. 'All the time we've been here I've only seen two snakes—and one of them was already dead. You don't run through long grass where you can't see what's under your feet, that's all. And sharks? All the beaches have spotters and lifeguards on duty. The minute there's a sighting they sound off a hooter and clear everybody out of the water in seconds. It's only happened three times to us, and one of those turned out to be a false alarm.'

'It sounds an idyllic kind of life,' Regan commented.

'Yeah,' he said thoughtfully. 'The main thing is to be adaptable. No good coming out here and expecting it to be like England.' He peered upwards at the rapidly clearing sky. 'Looks like it's over. We'll get you where you're going.'

The hotel was the same one she had left three days before, her room identical in everything but number. Looking out of the window on a scene already becoming familiar, Regan wondered how Keir had felt on first arriving in this new world, how long it had taken him to become accustomed to the differences. Perhaps for him the adjustment had been relatively easy. It was people like herself who found things difficult. Not that it mattered, as she was planning neither on staying nor on coming back, but it was interesting to conjecture how it might have been under other circumstances. All things considered, she was probably well out of it.

She was kidding herself, and she knew it. Given the right kind of encouragement, she would settle for this, or any other part of the world Keir happened to fancy. It wasn't where you were but who you were with that counted the most. Without Keir there was nothing for her anywhere.

She spent the next couple of days doing all the things a tourist would normally do—exploring the city districts on foot and by bus, cruising the Harbour by ferry, touring the Opera House complex to marvel along with so many hundreds of others at the sheer dramatic impact of Utzon's inspiration.

On the Friday she took a trip out to historic Botany Bay, crossing the causeway to visit the Bare Island museum and muse on days long gone when Captain Cook's *Endeavour* had ridden at anchor out there on the water, feeling somehow closer to home because of it. There was so much about this land that was different, yet so many of its people were of the same blood as herself. It was the first time she had really thought about it like that.

By Friday evening she was more than ready for Keir's return. No matter what heartache his presence elicited it had to be better than this solitary existence. Four more days and she would be back in England. Five, perhaps six, and he would be out of her life for ever. At least then she might be able to start putting herself back in order.

The phone call came through around five as she was contemplating whether to have dinner in her room and an early night or make a push and take herself out for a last look at the city by night. Don sounded pleased with himself.

'I worked out it would probably be one of three hotels if you were still in Sydney at all,' he said. 'This was the first try. When did you leave Keir's place?'

'The day he left for Brisbane,' Regan told him, trying to sound casual about it. 'He brought his schedule forward.'

'So I gathered. When does he get back?'

'Tomorrow.'

'Then Sunday's still on.' The pause was brief. 'You'll be staying till then?'

'I go home on Monday,' she said. 'I'm not sure I'll have time to get to the beach.'

'In that case, we'd better say our goodbyes tonight. You have nothing on?'

'No,' she was bound to admit, 'but——'

'No buts. I'll meet you at eight in the lobby.' He rang off before she could summon any further protest.

So what harm could it do? she reasoned. At least it was one way of passing the evening. Anything had to be better than spending another one alone.

Don was waiting when she got downstairs on the hour. Tonight he was wearing a suit and a tie, his pale blue shirt crisp at the collar.

'Horses for courses,' he quoted, registering her glance. 'I've got the car outside.'

They didn't have far to go, the restaurant he had chosen being only a couple of streets away. Seated at the window table, Regan looked out over the scintillating city to the fairytale span of the Harbour Bridge outlined against the sky.

'Beautiful,' she said. 'It really is beautiful!'

'Not bad,' Don agreed with typical Australian understatement. 'Do you want a drink before we eat?'

She shook her head, studying him across the lamplit table. 'Why did you go to so much trouble to contact me?'

His grin was disarming. 'I was at a loose end, for one thing, and I never got your home address, for another.'

'You could have asked Keir.'

'Except that I've a feeling you're one subject he won't want mentioning for some time to come.' He lifted a quizzical eyebrow at her lack of response. 'Not rising to it? Don't blame you. Anyway, if you're going home Monday you must have straightened things out.'

'Yes,' said Regan, 'we've straightened things out.' Her tone was dismissive. 'Why do you want my address?'

'So I can look you up when I come over.'

'You're thinking of doing that?'

'Could be. I've been offered an assignment for a series of articles on points of origin. Thought you might like to offer some typical British hospitality.'

She met his eyes levelly. 'I'd be delighted, except that there's a very good chance I'll be moving soon.'

'I wasn't talking about moving in with you, just visiting rights. You'll be leaving a forwarding address, I imagine.'

'I imagine I shall.' She gave him a bright smile. 'Do you have anything I can write on?'

Ron handed over a small pocket notebook and pen, and watched while she wrote, taking the paper from her to scan the few lines with a sudden upsurge of interest. '*Manor*, eh? Are you one of those impoverished rich we keep reading about?'

Her laugh held little amusement. 'If I was I'd hardly be wandering halfway round the world—unless you imagine I came to tap Keir for a loan.'

'It might have crossed my mind for a minute,' he responded, quite unabashed. 'He's in the right position.' His eyes wandered over her expensively simple tan silk dress and crinkled at the corners. 'Can't say you look so poor, though.'

'I'm not,' she assured him dryly. 'Doesn't that journalistic sense of yours ever take a rest?'

'I already told you it isn't a professional interest. It just intrigues me to know what would bring a girl like you eleven thousand miles for only a few days. And don't bother trying to make out you've been in Australia some time the way you did on Sunday. I went to the trouble of checking the incoming passenger lists for the weekend.' The pause was timed. 'As another matter of interest, I checked Monday's outgoing list too after I phoned you this afternoon, and found Keir's name on it as well as yours. Any comment on that?'

'None that need concern you.' Regan met his gaze without wavering. 'Did you hound your wife this way?'

His grimace held sudden wry humour. 'Just trying to make out how clear the field's going to be if and when I do come over.'

'He won't be staying,' she said. 'He should be back inside the week.' She lightened her tone with some deliberation. 'I gather the sabbatical isn't proving too fruitful?'

'You mean the book?' He shrugged. 'It's coming along.'

'Well enough for you to leave it alone for a while?'

'Probably not, but this job's too good to miss out on. The bank balance isn't lasting out the way I hoped.' He looked round as a waiter approached. 'Are you ready to order?'

When he wasn't delving into matters which didn't concern him, Don would be an entertaining companion, Regan found over the next couple of hours or so. All the same, she was glad when the time came to leave. If he did contact her in England she would find some way of putting him off, she decided on the way back to her hotel. She wanted no reminders of this period of her life.

Surprisingly he accepted her disinclination to adjourn to the hotel bar for a last drink with good grace.

'Had too many late nights myself,' he admitted. 'I'm going to need to be on top form to beat Keir on Sunday. Think you might make it after all?'

'I'll try,' she promised, with no real intention. 'It all depends.'

'I won't ask on what.' His grin was only faintly rueful. 'Sorry if I opened my mouth too wide. Bad habit of mine!'

He was gone before she could find any adequate reply to that.

Regan spent Saturday lazing around the hotel pool in a shade temperature of eighty-five, too lethargic to bother with any lunch. Going up to her room for a shower around three, she wondered what time Keir would get back and whether he would come downtown or not, unable to decide which course of action she would prefer. Monday was going to be difficult regardless: twenty-three hours in the close confines of a 747 was enough to tax the most stable of relationships. She had neither expected nor wanted Keir to pay for the tickets, but she knew better than to offer him the cost. It was his way of keeping control of the situation.

She was just about to step under the shower when the telephone started ringing. Heart beating appreciably faster, she went over to lift the bathroom extension, ridiculously selfconscious in her nudity.

'I've just got back,' Keir announced on a hard note. 'When did you leave?'

Regan made her own voice as expressionless as she was able. 'Wednesday, right after Leonie went. You didn't expect me to stay on there alone, did you?'

'From you,' he said, 'I should know better than to expect anything. I take it you'd prefer to stay where you are until we leave?'

More than forty hours, Regan calculated dully. Forty long and lonely hours. 'Yes,' she said.

'It's probably for the best.' The irony came across

loud and clear. 'How about tomorrow? Think you can stand a day on the beach, or did you have other plans made?'

Resolve gave way to the stronger need. There was no way she could get through on her own. 'I don't have any other plans made.'

'Then I'll pick you up around eight-thirty.' He seemed to hesitate for a brief moment as if about to say something else, then abruptly the receiver was replaced.

There had been long-drawn-out evenings and nights before, but that Saturday was the worst Regan had ever known. She was up before dawn, packing away all her things apart from those she would need for today and tomorrow. Exactly one week had passed since she had landed here in Sydney; it seemed more like a year. How the weeks and months to come were going to seem she hated to think. She would get through them because she had to, but it wasn't going to be easy.

She had coffee and toast brought to the room at seven-thirty, afterwards getting into a matching bikini and dress set which would serve throughout the day. By a quarter past eight she was down in the lobby, dark glasses at the ready for the moment Keir walked through the swing doors. It was the only way she was going to be able to face him with any equanimity.

He arrived at twenty-five minutes past the hour, lean and vital in the faded jeans and sweat shirt and making no attempt to touch her in any way as he walked her out to the car.

'We're going south,' he said briefly, sliding into the driving seat. 'The others will already be there. Got everything you need?'

Regan nodded, feeling the tension curling inside her as he put out a strong brown hand to the ignition. It was going to be worse even than she had imagined, every moment he made a tug at her senses. Never again to feel those hands on her body, the touch of his lips, to know the wild intoxication his lovemaking could bring. There were other men in the world, true, but none quite like Keir. If only she could go back, have her time over again. Yet would it be any better if she did? Without prior knowledge she would no doubt make exactly the same mistakes.

'How did the trip go?' she asked, doing her best to sound cool and composed. 'Successful, I hope?'

'Very.' He kept his eyes on the road ahead, his tone not particularly forthcoming. 'We're going to need to expand to keep pace.'

'We?'

'The Company. I got my board of directors together last night and dumped it in their laps for the next week.'

Regan bit her lip. 'It isn't a good time to be leaving, is it?'

His shrug was no denial. 'My presence isn't so crucial. Don't worry, I shan't let you down.'

The temptation to tell him there and then that she had changed her mind about asking him to return to England with her was strong, but she resisted it. At all costs she had to preserve the same image. Any change would elicit the obvious question of why, and that was one question she did not want to answer.

They reached their destination just before nine-thirty, one of many vehicles on the coastal highway. The long curve of beach was already crowded, the sea a deep dancing blue beyond the surf line. A big wave was racing shorewards carrying a dozen or more passengers on its crest.

'Leave your things in the car,' Keir advised, stripping off his shirt as he spoke. 'Easier than leaving them kicking around the beach.'

Regan unbuttoned her dress slowly, willing herself not to turn a hair when he got out of the car to take off his slacks and fling them on the rear seat. All around them others were doing the same, and with as little selfconsciousness. She used the wide soft belt of her dress as a bandeau to tie back her hair, leaving the ends to float free across her shoulders.

Keir had his board off the rack and slung over a shoulder by the time she was ready to go. He didn't look at her, turning to lead the way over the shallow stretch of scrubby duneland between the parking area and the beach proper.

'Over there,' he indicated, scanning the stretch of beach to the right. 'Looks like most of the crowd made it.'

Regan followed the tall, muscular figure as he threaded his way between supine bodies and scattered family groups, devouring the lines of his body with the eyes of one from whom such privilege was soon to be taken for ever. If this was the last occasion of its kind then let it be a good one, she thought. Forget what was past and gone, just live for today.

She recognised most of the people at present gathered in a large, loose circle, and was recognised herself with varying degrees of surprise.

'I thought you were only staying a few days,' remarked Jane Denver, looking up from the surfboard she was industriously waxing. Her smile was faintly edged. 'Finding it hard to leave us?'

'I go tomorrow,' Regan admitted. 'If I'd known you were going to be here I'd have asked Keir to bring your bikini along.'

'Oh, I'll pick it up some time.' She sounded unconcerned. 'Are you going to try surfing?'

Regan laughed and shook her head. 'I don't think so, thanks. Not this time.'

'Does that mean you'll be coming back another time?' Perhaps fortunately Jane didn't wait for any answer, drawing her own conclusions to judge from the glance she sent winging in Keir's direction. 'Better not leave it too long.'

'No.' Regan was thankful he was out of earshot. The young woman he was taking with was almost as tall as he was, and built in proportion except for shoulder muscles any man might have envied.

'Shirley Johnson,' supplied Jane without being asked. 'She's our great white hope for the next Olympics. You'd never believe she's only just seventeen, would you?'

'No,' Regan agreed, and hazarded a guess. 'A swimmer?'

'Butterfly and backstroke.' Jane carried on waxing her board. 'Which sports are you interested in?'

'Well—I play tennis.'

'Any good?'

'Fair.'

It was Jane's turn to laugh. 'That's what Keir said when I asked him once. It turned out he plays like a pro!'

'Well, I don't,' Regan hastened to assure her. 'I play for pleasure, and I don't mind losing.'

'You wouldn't last five minutes over here with that attitude,' came the blunt rejoinder. 'We play to win— at everything.'

Don Crossman's arrival carrying his still dripping board saved Regan the necessity of finding some reply to that, if there was a reply. 'So you came after all,' he said, dropping the board and flopping down in the sand at her side. 'You didn't seem to sure on Friday night.'

Keir was closer now, and must have heard, yet he gave no sign. Why should he? Regan asked herself. There was no jealousy on his side. So far as he was concerned she was free to do as she liked.

'I couldn't miss the big contest,' she said lightly. 'Who's going to win?'

'That's what we're here to find out.' He was grinning, eyes glinting up at her. 'If I do I'll let you take me out to an English candlelit dinner for two when I come over.'

'Are you thinking of taking a trip to England, Don?' asked Jane on a note of interest. 'When?'

'Two or three weeks. I'm not all that sure yet.'

'On assignment?'

'Yes.'

She gave a long, heartfelt sigh. 'Some have all the luck! Why couldn't I have a job like that!'

'Because you're not cut out for it,' he returned equably.

'You ready?' asked Keir from somewhere behind Regan's left shoulder, and she felt her whole body jerk. 'Jane, how about you?'

The latter shook her head. 'I didn't finish waxing yet. You two go ahead. I'll catch another set.'

Both girls watched the two men walk together down the beach towards the sea, one dark, one fair, the skin of their backs the same mahogany colour sported by so many around them. Keir was the taller, but only by a bare inch, and Don's shoulders were just as broad, his waist and hips as narrow. Odd, Regan thought numbly, how one could set her on fire while the other left her almost completely cold. Why couldn't it have been the other way round? She knew she didn't mean that. She didn't want to be in love with Don, she just wanted to be out of love with Keir. Unfortunately nothing was that simple.

It took the two men quite a length of time to swim their boards out beyond the breakers. Somebody loaned Regan a pair of binoculars so that she could get a better view, but even then it was several moments before she finally focussed on the two she sought among the fourteen or fifteen riders waiting out there for a suitable wave. They were sitting astride their boards, sculling with their hands to keep themselves spaced and steady, glancing back over bronzed shoulders to judge the swells building behind them. Several Regan herself would have thought more than adequate to requirements they allowed to pass under them, although one or two others made attempts.

'They'll sit it out till they get the big one,' Jane advised, sensing her growing impatience. 'The bigger and faster it is, the more skill is needed to ride it—and that's what Don's after proving.'

'And Keir?' Regan asked, keeping the glasses to her eyes for fear of missing the moment. 'Does he have to prove he's the better surfer too?'

'I don't think he could really care less,' came the answer. 'Only Don would't let him off the hook. Aussies have to be better than Poms—it's a law of the land. If Keir wins today Don will insist on another chance to prove himself—and another after that.'

'You think Keir will win?'

'It's anybody's guess. They're both good.' Jane was watching the sea through narrowed eyes, looking beyond the paddlers. 'There's a three set getting up out there. They've seen it too. Look at the way they're spreading!'

Regan's eyes were fixed on one man, watching him come up on to his knees on the board, the play of muscle in his arms and shoulders, the stretched grin of his lips. He was in his element, oblivious to anything but the moments to come. It was the way she would remember him.

Most of the other riders were up and away now, but Keir and Don still hung back.

'They're waiting for number three,' said Jane, and was on her feet as she spoke, craning her neck to get a better sighting. 'Now!'

Regan had risen too, binoculars glued to her eyes, hands trembling in vicarious excitement. Keir was standing on the swift-running board, balancing and controlling with fluid movements of body and limbs, his whole being concentrated on staying with the wave, towering above and behind him, a seemingly vertical face of water tipped with white foam.

Now the crest was arching forwards, forming an almost perfect semi-spherical curve before beginning to collapse in on itself from the right, and Keir was running left away from it, racing the curl, knees bent, body leaning at a crazy angle as he coaxed maximum speed from the board beneath his feet, then swinging back across the face as the wave firmed up again, leaving the white water behind.

Regan scarcely knew whether to be glad or sorry when he finally made the shallows, dropping backwards over the crest into the sea beside the bobbing board and leaving the wave to spend itself against the beach. For whole moments there she had lived that exhilaration, had felt the wind in her face, the tang of salt water on her skin, but she had also sensed the danger too. The one, she supposed, was an essential part of the other.

'Who won?' she asked in sudden recollection of the contest between the two men. 'I can't even see Don.'

Jane laughed. 'Easy to see where your interest lies! Don didn't manage that second turn. He's on his way back out for another go. Not that it counts. Keir won that fair and square on every count. Here he comes now.'

Watching him swinging easily up the beach towards them, Regan would have given anything for the right to say 'that's my husband, and I'm proud of him'. No, not the right, she corrected herself immediately; she already had that. What she needed was the courage. If she had been honest with herself a week ago there might have been a chance for them. Not much of one perhaps, but enough to work at. Now there was nothing.

The others tossed casual comments as he passed, most of it derisive in the fashion of their race. Keir simply grinned in answer and came on to where Regan sat with Jane, dropping his board to the sand as Don had done earlier and joining them.

'Congratulations,' Regan forced herself to say. 'I don't know much about surfing, but it looked wonderful from here.'

'And she should know, considering she had the glasses on you the whole run,' put in Jane blandly. 'You showed Don a thing or two.'

'I picked up just a fraction ahead of him,' said Keir. 'It makes all the difference. What happened to him?'

'He fell off and went straight back out again. You know Don—never say finish. He'll want another run later, you realise.'

'Then he's going to be unlucky. I'll only be here another hour or so, then it's back to town.'

'On a Sunday?' Jane sounded positively shocked. 'Man, nobody works on a Sunday!'

'Needs must,' he came back, unmoved. 'Things to catch up on.'

'What's wrong with the rest of the week?'

'I shan't be here.'

'Another trip? That's crook.'

Keir was looking at Regan, expression indefinable. 'You don't have to leave at the same time. Don or one of the others will be only too glad to run you in to your hotel. I'll sling your things in Don's car.'

'Thanks.' There was little else she could say. If she did go back to town she would simply be alone again. Rather anything than that.

Jane glanced from one to the other of them with an odd expression, as if she found herself unable to quite make something out. 'Next time you come it will have to be for longer,' she said. 'When do you think it might be?'

Regan's shrug was as light as she could make it. 'Who knows? Maybe never.'

'But you must! Keir, you'll persuade her, won't you?'

He was lying on his back now, hands clasped comfortably behind his head, face upturned to the sun. 'Nobody persuades Regan to do anything,' he came back pleasantly. 'If she comes back here at all, it will be at her own choice. Let me know when you're ready to go out. I might come with you for a last run before I leave.'

'I'm ready now,' said Jane, coming up on her knees to adjust her bikini top. 'Let's go!'

Don was coming out of the water as they went in. Regan saw the two men pause to exchange a few words, then Don was making his way up the beach with his board balanced under one arm.

'All alone?' he commented lightly, reaching her.

'Hardly,' she returned equally lightly with a glance around the group. 'I'm afraid I didn't see your second run. How did you do?'

'Better than the one before, wouldn't you know it!' He sounded relatively unconcerned. 'Seems I'm going to have to wait for another shot at equalling the score. Keir just asked me if I'd run you back to town later. He's got some jobs he wants to clear up.'

'So I understand.' Regan's eyes were on the two bobbing heads alongside the floating boards as they breasted a wave. 'Didn't Jane's regular boy-friend come today?'

'Garry? I think that finished during this last week. They've been going downhill for some time now. Never really suited in the first place.' He wasn't looking at her, but his tone had subtly changed. 'You realise she's got an eye on Keir?'

'Not specially.' Regan silently congratulated herself on the steadiness of her voice. 'They make a good couple. You know, I think I'm going to have to find myself some shade. My skin still isn't acclimatised to this sun of yours.'

'Stay put,' he commanded. 'I'll rig something up. Can't have you travelling all that way with sunburn tomorrow.'

Where he obtained it she had no idea, but some moments later he returned carrying a beach umbrella, which he proceeded to erect to the accompaniment of good-natured ribaldry from those around them. By the time Keir and Jane returned to the group, Regan was ostensibly dozing beneath it. She heard Keir say something about not bothering to disturb her, and opened her eyes in time to see his back disappearing in the direction of the parking area. So that was that. When she saw him again she would be on her way home.

The rest of the day went by surprisingly swiftly. Around two the whole crowd adjourned a few kilometres down the coast for a lunch which lasted till teatime, afterwards moving back to Sydney en masse to finish up at someone's home in the suburbs for an impromptu party at which male and female members soon became separate groups.

'You'll not pull Don out of there for at least another couple of hours,' advised Jane when Regan began showing signs of restlessness around ten. 'I'm ready to go myself. How about I drop you off?'

Regan had no hesitation in accepting the offer. She was tired after the long day in the open, and the last thing she wanted was another session of leave taking from Don. She asked one of the other girls to tell him thanks from her, and went out with Jane to the little saloon parked way down at the end of a row of others all bearing the same surfboard mascot.

'I hadn't realised you were driving your own car,' she said, sliding into the front seat. 'I suppose I just

took it for granted you'd come with one of the others.'
She hesitated before adding, 'Don told me you'd
broken up with your regular boy-friend. Is it final?'

'For both of us,' Jane returned levelly. 'It's been
coming for weeks.' She put the car into motion, drawing out from the kerbside. 'He plays rugby football,
which I hate, and he doesn't have any interest in surfing or any other water sport. I'd say we did well to last
as long as we did.'

Regan said softly, 'Next time you'll have to find a
man who shares the same interest.'

'Yes.' The blonde head turned briefly. 'I admit Keir
would be the obvious target if he was free.'

Regan's heart contracted. 'What makes you think he
isn't?'

'Instinct. I'm not sure what it is between you two,
but there's something.'

Regan was silent for a long moment. 'I'm going
home tomorrow,' she pointed out at length.

'And he's going with you,' Jane cut in before she
could add anything else. 'Don told me.'

'He had no right!'

'Don doesn't worry about rights. He likes making
ripples and standing back to watch how they grow. I
gather it's true anyway.'

Regan sighed. 'Yes. But he'll only be in England a
few days, then he'll be back.'

'And you won't be coming with him?'

'No.' She made a small helpless gesture. 'I'm sorry,
I can't explain the situation. If you want to know more
you'll have to ask Keir himself.'

'I might do that when he does get back.'

Both girls were quiet after that. It wasn't until they
were saying their goodbyes outside Regan's hotel that
Jane said unexpectedly, 'You know, there'd be no hard
feelings if you did decide to come with him. There are
other men.'

She would try and remember that latter advice, Regan thought as the car moved off again. Perhaps one day she might even find one who could make her forget Keir. At least it was something to hope for.

The red light was lit on the telephone indicating a message awaiting her. The switchboard operator read it out for her. Mr Anderson was to pick her up at ten-thirty. Just that, nothing more. Regan wondered dully how many times he had telephoned, and what he had thought of her continued absence. Yet if she had been here what good would it have done? It was over and finished, and she had to accept it.

CHAPTER ELEVEN

THEY landed at Heathrow in pouring rain after a journey lasting almost thirty hours owing to a hold-up in Bangkok, to find unreserved hire cars at a premium. It took Keir some half an hour to secure the Renault which was all that was available, and even with the driving seat right to the back of the ratchet he looked far from comfortable behind the wheel.

Regan's offer to do the driving was somewhat brusquely turned down. 'It's my own fault for not booking one through from Sydney,' he said, 'so I'll put up with it. We'll just have to stop more often to stretch our legs.'

Regan seized her opportunity at the first of those stops to phone through to Cottam and inform a surprised Sullivan that they were on their way.

'Have one of the guestrooms prepared for Mr Anderson,' she told him unemotionally. 'He won't be staying very long. We're going to have lunch on the way, so you don't need to bother.'

'Everything okay?' Keir asked when she got back to the car. 'The house hasn't burned down or anything?'

'Not unless Sullivan forgot to mention it,' she came back smartly, and at once regretted the loss of control. 'We're both tired,' she said, striving for a more reasonable note. 'Can't we forget about all that for the time being?'

The glance he gave her had a curious quality. 'All right, it's forgotten. Any particular place you fancy stopping for lunch?'

She shook her head. 'Right now I don't even feel

much like eating. We seem to have been on the move for days.'

'You'll probably feel better with something on your stomach,' he said. 'You didn't eat any breakfast on the plane.' He started the engine without waiting for an answer. 'I'll use my own judgment.'

They stopped eventually at a pub restaurant somewhere off the M1 close to Woburn Abbey and ate an indifferent meal which left neither of them feeling very much better. There was little conversation when they got on the way again. Regan could feel her eyes closing, and fought to keep awake, aware that Keir must be just as tired. Eventually she could stave it off no longer, head lolling against the doorpost as she fell into a bottomless pit of exhaustion.

It was still raining when she awoke what seemed like only minutes later, but there was a familiarity about the passing scenery which brought her head swiftly upright.

'We're only about ten miles from Cottam!' she exclaimed disbelievingly. 'I can't have slept all *that* time!'

'You did,' Keir assured her. 'Very soundly. Why worry? Best thing you could have done.'

'I could have taken a spell at the wheel,' she came back, 'and given you a chance to sleep. You should have woken me.'

His lips moved with faint humour. 'Who's to say I'd have slept anyway with a woman at the wheel? This isn't one of your smooth automatics.'

'I can drive a geared car,' she retorted, but her heart wasn't in it. 'Thanks anyway. My neck feels as stiff as a board, but at least I can think straight again.'

'I'm glad one of us can.' He took a hand off the wheel to run it around the back of his own neck, easing the strained muscles. 'First thing I'm going to need is a good hot bath, then a bed in a darkened room with a "do not disturb" sign on the door.'

'It's all been arranged.' She was looking out of the window, thinking how little real time had passed since the day she had first seen Keir again. Just three short weeks, that was all. Three weeks to bring them to this. Soon it would be spring, the beginning of all things new. But not for them. It was already too late.

Driving up to the house she was able to view it dispassionately for the very first time, acknowledging the waste. She wouldn't sell it, she would give it away to some deserving cause; if necessary even set up a maintenance fund too. A convalescent home for sick children; she liked the sound of that. Cottam should have the family her father had wanted for it. Matt would know how to set the ball rolling. There were rules and regulations even governing free gifts. But whatever it cost to set up it was going to happen; on that she was quite determined.

Sullivan met them at the door, his greeting as circumspect as ever. Tea was ready any time they wanted it, he told them. Should he serve it right away or would they prefer to wait?

'What I'd prefer is a large whisky,' Keir told him bluntly. 'If you'd like to bring it upstairs to the bathroom. I'm going to soak for half an hour, then sleep for however long it takes to bring me round, so I shan't be wanting anything else for some time. Just point me in the right direction.'

'I'll show you,' said Regan. 'Sullivan can get the whisky.' She was moving towards the stairs as she spoke, limbs suddenly heavy again. 'I think I might follow your example. There's time enough tomorrow for everything else.'

The room prepared for Keir was at the far end of the gallery from her own. She stayed in the doorway as he walked in to dump the suitcases he had insisted on carrying up himself on the ottoman at the foot of the bed, hands tightly curled in the pockets of her cream wool dress.

'I hope you'll be comfortable,' she said. 'You've your own bathroom, through there.'

'With terms on the back of the door?' He turned to look at her, lips twisting as he did so. 'You don't have to play the good hostess for me, I'm only your husband. I'll see you later.'

Regan left him then, going along to her own room and closing the door softly behind her. Another minute back there and she would have been finished. Tired and drawn as he was, she had never loved or wanted him more. What would he have done, she wondered, had she given way to impulse and gone to him just now? Would he have held her close the way she had wanted him to, or simply thrust her impatiently away? She would never know, because the moment had passed. She doubted if there would be another.

The room was dark when she awoke, and for a moment she imagined herself back in Sydney. The luminous hands of her bedside clock said it was just after midnight. That seemed about par for the course. It would be at least a couple of days before she got back into a regular pattern again.

Getting up, she went to the window, drawing back the curtains a little way to look out on the coldly-lit grounds. It would be ten o'clock in the morning in Sydney now, and hot, the distances shimmering and hazy. They had winter too, of course, but it was hardly the same. The days would grow cooler, but the sun would still be there.

And Keir. Who would he be with by then? Jane? Perhaps. They went well together. Naturally she would have to know the truth. How would she take it? Philosophically, Regan imagined. Two years wasn't so long to wait for a man like Keir.

She was hungry, she realised suddenly. As it was more than twelve hours since she had eaten that was hardly surprising. One thing was certain, she wasn't going to get back to sleep for a while yet, so she might as well go and find herself some food.

The kitchen was on the east side of the house, big and modern and clinically clean. Regan put on one of the concealed unit lights at the side of the refrigerator, reluctant to flood the place with the three overhead tubes. Her father had brought in the best and most expensive kitchen fitters he could find at the time of renovation, but though the finished result was certainly efficient and easy to run, it lacked any element of homeliness. The kitchen at Keir's place was modern too, yet the materials used had given it warmth and welcome. How Mrs Sullivan could create the dishes she did create in this atmosphere was beyond her.

There was no shortage of food in the refrigerator. Regan took out a half chicken and carved several slices from the breast, then split a couple of bread rolls to make thick sandwiches. Some coffee now to go with them and she would be all set. She should have put the kettle on first, of course, then it would have been boiling by now, but logical thought didn't come easy to one unaccustomed to fending for herself.

She was waiting for the kettle to come to the boil and nibbling at the edge of a roll when the door opened again slowly. Keir had on a short terry robe and nothing else, if the bare legs beneath were anything to go by.

'I had the same idea,' he said. 'My stomach woke me up grumbling at the lack of sustenance. What are you having?'

'Chicken,' she said. 'There's plenty more if you'd like some.'

He came over to open the refrigerator door, the thin leather slippers making little sound against the tiled floor. 'Beef's more my style. Where do you keep the carving knives?'

Regan put a hand to the unit top behing her and drew out the one she had used, unable to stop herself tensing a little when his fingers touched hers in taking it from her. He must have felt it in her, but he said nothing, his face too far above the radius of the down-shaded light to reveal any subtle change of expression. The hiss of escaping steam from the kettle was a relief.

By the time she had made two mugs of coffee, he had his own sandwiches ready stacked, the thinly sliced beef oozing out of every side. Regan had intended carrying her booty back to her room with her, but to go now would be tantamount to making an escape. She took a stool opposite him at the central console table, switching on the suspended light which played only over the surface, leaving the two of them in shadow.

'The last time I ate a midnight feast was when I was at the Poly,' he remarked, biting into one of the sandwiches with relish. 'There were four of us sharing a small flat, but we were always chronically short of money. I got myself an evening job washing up in a café, with a meal thrown in as part of my wages. Strictly off the record, naturally. Moonlighting was banned.'

'You had a grant, surely?' Regan asked, and felt rather than saw his mouth curl.

'Sure I had a grant. And I'm not knocking it either. It just needed supplementing, that's all. Some got the extra through their family, but mine couldn't afford any hand-outs. Hence the job. Others did it too.'

She was silent, seeing in her mind's eye the young Keir, poor and proud with it. He had probably been making a fair salary by the time she got to know him—by his own standards at least. Certainly the places he had taken her had not been so cheap. He had been able to run a car, to afford decent clothes, perhaps even put something by for the future. Yet none of it had been enough for her. She hadn't known then what love was about.

'What are you thinking about?' he asked quietly, and for once she found herself answering without prevarication.

'The night we first met. I remember how tall you were, and how confident.'

'Too confident,' he rejoined. 'I thought at the time that was all it took.'

'Until I disillusioned you.' She put the half-eaten roll back on the plate, suddenly not hungry any more. 'I'm going back to bed.'

He caught her wrist as she came round the console to pass him, turning on the revolving stool to draw her to him. 'I'm still confident in one thing,' he murmured thickly. 'I want you, Regan. Now. Tonight. I don't care how much it confuses the issue.'

'No!' Her own voice sounded hoarse. 'I don't——'

'You do. You did when I touched you just now. If it's all we've got why not make the most of it while we can?'

Whatever answer she might have made to that was cut off by the pressure of his mouth on hers, and then it was too late. She made no attempt to struggle free as he lifted her up off the floor and carried her from the room, her face turned into the soft towelling of his robe, smelling the male scent of him. He had carried her like this once before, only then she had been fighting him. Let tonight be different. Let it be the way it should have been then. It was going to have to last her a long time, this memory.

Keir took her to her own room, laying her gently down on the bed. When he switched out the light it was as if he had read her mind. She needed darkness as a cloak, not for her body but for her emotions. He undressed her slowly, kissing her throat, her breasts, murmuring words she couldn't hear against her warm skin. Then he took off his robe and came down beside her, gathering her into his arms to hold her close while his fingertips explored the length of her spine, tracing the curve of her hip, drifting across her waist and back to where they had begun their journey, his weight coming over her so gradually she only felt it at the last moment before he claimed her.

Weak sunlight was filtering into the room through the curtains she had left partially opened when she awoke again. She was alone in the bed, the pillow beside her head undisturbed. For a numb moment she wondered if she could have dreamed the events of the night, but the swollen tenderness of her mouth was all it took to convince her that it had been real enough. They had made love more than once, each time more fulfilling than the last, yet not fulfilling enough apparently to stop Keir from leaving her in the cold light of day. He had even had the decency to plump up the other pillow in case Sullivan should bring her breakfast in bed. She must remember to thank him for that gesture.

She knew she would do no such thing. What had passed between them last night was to be ignored, relegated to its proper place: a temporary madness now appeased. Today would see the end of their relationship to all intents and purposes. Once Keir had signed that damned paper of her father's they would both be free to go their own ways. At least she still had her pride intact. She had not been betrayed into telling him she loved him. It was small consolation, but she was grateful for it.

Looking at the clock she found it was already gone nine. No doubt Sullivan had hesitated to disturb the sleepers, especially realising as he must that they had been down for a snack in the night. Was Keir in his room she wondered, or had he gone running? Clearing his head for the day to come. She had to do that herself. No use standing around looking as desolate as she felt.

Keir had had all he wanted from her last night.

She was showered and dressed when the phone started ringing. Fiona sounded warm and happy. 'So you managed it,' she said. 'Sullivan told me you'd arrived. It didn't take long, did it? I knew all he needed was convincing.'

'He isn't staying,' Regan said plainly because she saw no point in prevarication. 'He only came to sign a paper Matt has waiting. How are things at the shop?'

The silence at the other end seemed way out of proportion both in length and depth. When Fiona spoke again it was on a note totally alien to her normally effervescent nature. 'The shop is doing fine. Regan, I have to talk to you.'

'It's going to have to wait,' she said. 'I'm getting Matt out here first thing.'

'Matt isn't here. In town, I mean. He was called away on family business. I think his brother is very ill.'

'Oh?' Regan felt quite blank. 'You don't know when he's likely to be back?'

'I don't know anything. I only happened to hear about it.' She paused, before adding slowly, 'It isn't going to make any difference anyway.'

'What's that supposed to mean?'

'It's what I wanted to talk to you about. And I can't do it over the phone.' The tone firmed again in resolution. 'I'm coming over there.'

Regan stayed in her room until she arrived, afraid of running into Keir before she had this thing sorted out. Recalling Matt's discomfiture when he had come to see her that day, she was already beginning to suspect the truth, and it sickened her. How did she go about telling Keir he had come all this way on a wild goose chase? Why should he even believe her? He would take it she had tricked him into coming back to Cottam with her, and there was only one reason she would have done that. So much for her pride!

Fiona confirmed the suspicion as fact within two minutes of entering the room, her spirits dampened to an extent Regan would not have believed under normal circumstances.

'I persuaded Matt Swain to do what he did,' she claimed. 'He didn't much like the idea, but he agreed because I convinced him it was the only way to make you go after Keir. I thought if the two of you just got together again away from Cottam it would all come right. I'm only sorry it didn't work out that way.'

Regan was sitting on the window seat, face turned towards the hills. 'So all I ever needed was the marriage certificate itself,' she said huskily. 'It's all been for nothing. What on earth do I tell him?'

'Would you like me to tell him I was the culprit?' Fiona asked. 'So I made a mistake. Surely he'll——' She stopped there, her eyes on Regan's face, registering the sudden contraction about her mouth. 'But I didn't make any mistake, did I?' she said softly. 'You wanted him back. Did you tell him that?'

'No.'

'Why not?'

'Because he has his own life out there and he doesn't need me in it.' Her head came round, her lips fixed now in a strained little smile. 'He doesn't *need* me, Fi.'

They were still gazing helplessly at each other when the knock came at the door. Expecting Sullivan with some food, Regan called out an invitation, freezing when Keir appeared. He was wearing slacks and a sweater, the dampness of his hair testifying to a recent shower. He paused when he saw Fiona, his expression undergoing an indefinable alteration.

'Sorry,' he said, 'I didn't realise you had company.' His smile was for the other girl, easy and casual. 'How are you?'

'Rotten,' she stated without equivocation. 'I'm glad

you put in an appearance, Keir. It saves me having to search you out. I'm afraid I've a confession to make.'

Regan was on her feet, face flushed but decisive 'Just leave it, will you? I'll do my own explaining.'

Keir looked from one to the other, eyes narrowed a little. 'Explain what?' he demanded.

'That I was the one who put Matt Swain up to all that rigmarole about needing your signature,' Fiona got in before Regan could speak again. 'You see, I had it all wrong. I thought it was only pride that was keeping you two apart. I thought if you once got together again you'd sort it all out. Instead it seems all I've done is bring you all the way back here for nothing.' She spread her hands, expression rueful. 'What can I say except sorry?'

'Not a lot,' he agreed dryly. 'At least the intention was good.' His eyes moved back to Regan, cool and impenetrable. 'I see it's been a shock for you too. All that wasted effort! Good thing I didn't bother unpacking.'

'I'm going,' Fiona said swiftly. 'Regan, I'll see you tomorrow.' She moved to the door, shoulders lifting in an apologetic little shrug as Keir shifted to let her through. 'In future I'll keep my nose out of other people's affairs.'

'It might be best,' he responded. He shut the door again after she had gone, leaning his weight against it as he looked across at Regan. 'So Cottam is yours regardless. Congratulations. Pity you didn't know it last night. You could have saved yourself the humiliation.'

She stared at him across the width of the room, eyes bright blazing green in the whiteness of her face 'You're saying I only slept with you last night because I was afraid you might back out on the arrangement?'

'Not wholly, perhaps—I'll grant myself that much. The smile was slow and sardonic. 'But I doubt if you'd have been quite so—forthcoming, shall we say?—if you hadn't believed the Manor might be at stake.'

The emotions churning inside her crystallised suddenly into one searing flash of anger and hurt. 'Damn the Manor! And damn you too, Keir! Just get out of here, will you? Go back to where you came from! I'm not likely to come bothering you again.'

He didn't move, studying her with an odd expression. 'Say that again, will you? About Cottam.'

It was too late now to back out; she had given herself away. So let him have the triumph of knowing how she felt about him. What did it matter any more? 'I don't care about Cottam,' she said thickly. 'Ironical, isn't it? Six years ago you told me you loved me, and I laughed in your face. Well, now it's your turn to do the laughing. Only go and do it somewhere else, will you, because I don't think I can take it either.'

Still he made no move, gazing at her as if he'd never seen her before. 'I'm still not sure I've got it straight,' he said at last. 'Are you saying what you seem to be saying?'

'You mean you want me to spell it out for you.' Her laugh was bitter. 'Why not? It might even make the journey half worthwhile!' She put up a hand and pushed the hair from her forehead, head lifted with a touch of defiance. 'I came after you because I had to. Cottam was just an excuse. It took you just two days to make me fall in love with you. No—' she shook her head—'that's not strictly true either. I was never really out of love with you. Not in six years. It started again the moment I saw you in the café, only I didn't want to acknowledge it. Maybe Leonie was right, maybe I made you that offer in the hope that you'd do just as you did and refuse to take the money when the time came. What I didn't count on was your leaving me the way you did. I thought—I hoped——' she broke off, swallowing hard. 'Does it really matter what I thought? You paid me back, every last cent. More in fact, because what you did was calculated and what I did wasn't. I was young and spoiled and I hadn't had time to learn that there could be things in life more important than money and position. Well, I've learned now, and you can take the credit for having taught me. Better late than never, isn't that what they say?'

'Regan.' His voice was very soft; unbelievably tender. 'Stop it, darling. You're not the only one who never stopped loving. I thought I had. I thought I could use you the way you appeared to be using me again and go off without a pang. Only it didn't work out like that. Do you remember how you came on me that first day by the pool? I was thinking about you then, wondering if it was too late to come back and start over. Then I turned round and you were standing there, and for a wild moment I actually believed you felt the same way.'

'Until I ruined it all by flinging Cottam at your head again.' She was tremulous, still not wholly sure. 'If I'd waited just a moment would you have told me then how you felt?'

His smile came slow. 'I wouldn't have had to tell you. I was planning on showing you.'

Somehow she was across the room and in his arms, half laughing, half crying as she clung to him, her face against the strong deep chest. 'Oh, God, I've been such a fool!'

'I'm not especially proud of how I reacted,' Keir admitted, lips gently smoothing her temple. 'There was only one way I knew to get to you, and I intended taking full advantage of it.' He tipped up her chin to see her face, his smile a caress in itself. 'Only when it came right down to it I knew I wanted more than that from you. That's why I called in Leonie. Moral support.'

Regan put up her own hands to touch the lean, tanned face, tracing the line of his mouth with a finger and feeling the reaction deep within him. 'She knew I was in love with you. She told me so.'

'Then I wish she'd told me too,' he growled.

'Would you have believed her?'

'I might. Women are more sensitive to these things.' There were sparks in the greyness of his eyes, small dancing lights growing by the minute. She could feel the desire in him, see it in the curve of his mouth, the hardening of his jawline. When he kissed her it was roughly, lifting her as he did so to carry her to the bed.

'The door,' she said against his lips. 'Sullivan might come with breakfast for——'

He was gone before she completed the sentence, striding across to turn the key in the lock, then returning more slowly, shedding his clothing as he came. 'That takes care of Sullivan,' he said. 'Now I'll take care of you.'

If the night before had been fulfilling, this was infinitely more so, because for the first time they had nothing to hide. Cradling the weight of the dark head against her shoulder after that final, shattering climax, Regan thought dreamily of all the days and nights to come—of wakening each morning to the knowledge of a love shared, and still with room to grow. No more regrets for what might have been six years ago, because it could never have been like this. Never in a thousand years!

'About this place,' Keir murmured. 'Did you mean what you said?'

'I meant it.' Her voice was low, but it carried conviction. 'I'm afraid the Sullivans are just going to have to take what's been provided for them. They'll be very comfortable, I'll make sure of that.' She paused for a moment, fingers moving softly through the hair at the nape of his neck. 'What do you think about turning the house into a children's home—a convalescent home? We could set up a trust fund to help finance the running. After all, I'm hardly going to need all that money daddy left me, am I? Not with an engineering wizard for a husband.'

He lifted his head to look at her then, mouth faintly curved. 'I can keep the two of us in fair comfort, yes— even three or four as and when required. But it won't be here in England, Regan. I've made my home over there.'

'I know. And I'm not arguing.' She put a hand to each side of the strong face, lifting her own head to press a kiss to his lips. 'My home is where you are, be it Australia, China or Timbuctoo! I'd follow you to the ends of the earth.'

'Such devotion,' he mocked, but there was tenderness in his voice. 'Oh, God, I love you! And when I think how close I came to never saying it again.'

'And how close I came to never saying it at all,' she murmured. 'I was such a blind little idiot. I couldn't see beyond the end of my nose. How you must have despised me.'

'I didn't despise you. It wasn't your fault you were the way you were. It probably wouldn't have worked out even if you'd been otherwise inclined. Like you said once before, without the incentive I might never have made the push to start a new life, and you certainly wouldn't have been happy on what I could have offered you here in Cottam. You still wouldn't, if it came to that. Love can overcome a lot of differences, but it can't change basic nature. You belong in a certain setting, darling, and I'm glad I can give it to you.'

In her mind's eye, Regan saw the house overlooking the sea, felt the sun on her skin, the wind in her face. A new life, a different life, but one she already felt at home with.

'How soon can we go back?' she said.

THE FINE WHISKY OF SCOTLAND

More than five hundred years ago, Scotch whisky was the he-man's drink of Scotland's common folk. The companion to hard toil and exercise in the clear Highland air, *uisgebeatha*—Gaelic for "water of life"—was also the only drink served at weddings and wakes, and the *deoch an dorius*—"final door drink"—at parties.

In the Highlands of Scotland, among the misty mountains, the dark still lakes and the untamed rivers, the unique ingredients that go into the manufacture of Scotch whisky are found. Here the barley for the malt is grown, then sprouted for several days in water that has acquired a brownish color from flowing through the rich dark peat moss on the moors. The sprouted barley is then dried in a peat fire, and it is the acrid and oily smoke that give the whisky its characteristic aroma. The dried sprouts are mashed into a grist and soaked in hot water, producing a malt. When the water, or *wort*, has absorbed all the goodness of the malt, it is drained and fermented into beer. The beer is fermented three more times—during which process it is changed to a wine, then distilled to a liquor—before being drawn into casks and aged for anywhere from three to ten years.

When Keir, the hero of Kay Thorpe's novel, sits down to enjoy a glass of his favorite drink he undoubtedly heeds the advice of this Scottish saying: "There are two things a Scotsman likes naked, and one of them is Scotch." It is only by sipping Scotch whisky straight that one can fully enjoy the light smoky malt flavor that makes this liquor world renowned.

Take these 4 best-selling novels FREE

ANNE HAMPSON
gates of steel

ANNE MATHER
sweet revenge

VIOLET WINSPEAR
devil in a silver room

JANET DAILEY
no quarter asked